Toby Forward

WYVERN WINTER

Illustrated by
Michael Foreman

PUFFIN BOOKS

PUFFIN BOOKS

Published by the Penguin Group
Penguin Books Ltd, 27 Wrights Lane, London W8 5TZ, England
Penguin Books USA Inc., 375 Hudson Street, New York, New York 10014, USA
Penguin Books Australia Ltd, Ringwood, Victoria, Australia
Penguin Books Canada Ltd, 10 Alcorn Avenue, Toronto, Ontario, Canada M4V 3B2
Penguin Books (NZ) Ltd, 182–190 Wairau Road, Auckland 10, New Zealand

Penguin Books Ltd, Registered Offices: Harmondsworth, Middlesex, England

First published by Andersen Press Limited 1992
Published in Puffin Books 1994
1 3 5 7 9 10 8 6 4 2

Printed in England by Clays Ltd, St Ives plc
Filmset in Century Schoolbook

ONE

Miss Jane Gwyer stood stone-still as they pelted her with snowballs. Snow clung to the folds of her long skirt. Snow smashed into her high straight shoulders. Snow melted down the front of her old-fashioned jacket and trickled round and over the smooth buttons. Miss Gwyer's cheerful, determined face stared out over the village green, now newly white with overnight deep snow. The church stood anciently behind her. To

5

one side of the church, behind Miss Jane Gwyer's right shoulder, Wivern Manor scowled over the scene. The manor house, Miss Gwyer's house, looked on, shocked and angry, as the village children fired snowballs at her. But Miss Gwyer saw none of this. Her eyes stared blindly out from a face which, so far, had not been hit by snowballs.

'Go on! In her face,' Jack encouraged the others.

Thomas packed snow into a tight, hard ball, one that would really sting if it hit. He took aim at Miss Gwyer's calm face and flung it as hard as he could. It grazed the funny hat she wore, sprinkling a fine dust of snow on her shoulders, but spinning away uselessly.

'Rotten,' Jack judged it.

Towser, bewildered yet enthralled by the snow, yapped and snapped and bounded off to retrieve the snowball. His small legs with a spaniel's long fur sank into the deep drifts and he scrambled out. He rolled and leaped, sending billows of dry snow all over, lost in the joy of the strange cold. Neither he nor the children had ever seen snow before.

'Go on,' Jack repeated. His own snowball had fallen far too low and had struck Miss Gwyer in the stomach. Thomas missed again. Clare took careful aim, standing sideways on, then launched hers. It was not a hard throw and could

6

not have hurt like the sort of missile that Thomas discharged, but her snowball curved up and fell directly towards Miss Gwyer, landing full in her face. The snow exploded into a white cloud.

'Got her! Got her!' Jack crowed.

Thomas swivelled round and flung his snowball at random, having no interest in Miss Gwyer, now that Clare had won. It hit the huge board outside the manor that read: ACQUIRED FOR CLIENTS.

The tightly-packed ball slammed the board with a thud that shook the loose snow from its top edge and sent Towser plunging away yelping in surprise.

'Look,' called Clare.

The boys followed her pointing finger and squinted up at the top windows of the dark house. All was still and silent.

'What?' asked her brother.

'I saw someone,' Clare claimed, still pointing up. 'Up there.'

'No,' argued Thomas.

'Nothing there now,' Jack told his sister.

'No,' agreed Clare.

'Been empty for years,' Thomas persisted. 'Never anyone in there.'

'No,' agreed Clare. 'But look.' She indicated the board. 'Someone's bought it.

'Have they?'

'Yes. That's what that means. "Acquired for clients" means someone's bought it.'

'Why don't they say so?' asked Thomas. He was packing another of his very hard snowballs.

'What's a client?' Jack asked.

Clare ignored this difficult question. 'When you hit the board,' she said to Thomas, 'a face came in that window.'

'All right,' said Thomas. He grinned out from behind a mass of freckles. 'Watch the window.'

Clare and Jack looked up. Clare was two years younger than Jack but she was already as tall as her brother. With their dark eyes beneath thick black eyebrows and their straight black hair, they looked like twins.

Thomas threw the snowball as hard as he could. It banged against the board. Towser yapped and danced around, used to this game now.

'Nothing,' repeated Jack. 'It's empty.'

Thomas tried another. Then another. Soon, all three were hurling snow at the board until it was dotted with white marks. Towser loved it. He rolled in the snow beneath the board, waiting for another shower of fine white snow to spray on him. He leaped in the air, hopelessly too short to catch the balls in his mouth, but snapping at them all the same. Clare lobbed a few low ones from time to time to encourage him and give him something he could reach.

8

The echoes from the distant thudding trembled against the old windows of the house, sending vibrations of life and excitement through them. The thud, thud, thud suggested footsteps on the bare, dusty floorboards.

When the snowballs stopped, the thud, thud, thud continued inside. A face peered cautiously round the window frame and watched the three children and the dog walk past Miss Jane Gwyer, across the village green and into a small house.

Miss Gwyer, her back to the house and to the eyes that watched her, stared blindly at the children. The snow that clung to her in the cold air partly obscured the writing on the stone plinth on which she had stood for over a hundred and fifty years.

JANE GWYER
born 1743
who for twelve years was Mistress
of Wivern Manor, until her sudden
Disappearance in 1781. Mild of Manner,
yet she was Strong of Purpose, her
Desire always to Right wrongs. She
was Even-handed to Creatures of
Whatsoever Estate, Conscientious in
her Duty, Faithful and Obedient as a
Daughter, Condescending to the Poor,
unmoved by the Pretentions of
the Great.

All Creatures of the Hearth and
Beasts of the Wild were her
Friends and knew no Fear where
she was, or where
She Is Now.

Underneath this message was carved the image of a winged dragon, with feet like an eagle and a barbed serpent's tail.

TWO

A second pair of eyes watched the children. Sharp eyes in a keen face. These eyes had watched them pelting the statue. And these eyes had caught the small movement in the upper window of Wivern Manor.

'There's someone in there,' she said to Shakti. 'They've arrived.'

Shakti slithered round Felicity Aylmer's neck and slid through her hands, his shiny scales

11

warm to her touch. Miss Aylmer let the snake find a comfortable place, then raised his head to look at hers. 'It's beginning,' she said.

Shakti hissed.

'I'm glad you agree.' She smiled.

Shakti curved his long body and slid away from her, dropping to the floor.

'Toast,' said Clare, sniffing as they walked in.

'Wrong,' said her mother.

'Smells good,' said Jack. 'What do you think?'

Thomas looked at Mrs Roberts.

'There's plenty,' she said. 'You'll stay and have some?'

'Well, if that's all right. I don't want to take your tea.' His auburn hair fell over green eyes, hiding him from the offer.

Clare pushed him forward into the room. 'Take your shoes off.' She was already slipping off her wet shoes.

'Thanks. It's crumpets,' he said.

Jack launched himself at Towser in delight. The dog side-stepped and Jack went hurtling on to a sofa.

'Careful,' warned his mother. 'You'll break something.'

'Is it? Is it crumpets?'

Thomas and Clare sat near the fire.

'It's nothing for you if you don't get those wet shoes off this minute,' his mother warned him.

'How's things, Thomas?'

Thomas smiled but did not let his eyes meet hers. 'Oh, fine,' he said. 'Good.'

'And your mother?'

Thomas held his hands to the fire, palms forward. 'She's a lot better.'

Mrs Roberts produced a huge blue and white china dish, piled high with crumpets. 'Three each to start with, so you needn't grab and you needn't fight over them.'

'I don't know why you're looking at me like that,' said Jack. 'It's Clare who eats most.' He took two at once.

Clare took one and tore it in half before she bit it.

'If there's anything I can do,' said Mrs Roberts to Thomas again, 'tell your mum she just has to say so.'

Thomas nodded. 'She's been a lot better,' he said, 'since the operation.'

'Right. I'm glad. But all the same. Don't forget.'

'I won't,' said Thomas, and he let himself look at her directly for a moment.

'Don't give Towser all your crumpet, Clare,' she said. 'They clog him up.'

'Why don't they clog us up?' asked Jack.

'There's someone in the Manor,' said Clare. 'I saw them.'

'No, she didn't,' said Jack. 'Trick of the light.

'What will happen to it?' asked Thomas.

'I don't know,' said Mrs Roberts. 'I can't think who could afford to buy a great place like that.'

'Film star,' said Clare.

'Pop star,' said Jack, pretending to play a guitar.

'More likely a school,' said their mother.

'A school?' said Clare.

'Why not? Plenty of room there. More likely than a person wanting to live in it.'

The three children looked at each other in surprise.

'You mean we'll go there? Instead of on the bus to Barrowdale?'

The three were the only children in the village and were collected with others by a special bus that went round the villages picking up children to take them to school.

'No. Not a village school, a boarding school.'

'You mean the village will be full of other children? All living here, in the Manor? Great.' Jack bit hard into another crumpet.

'I don't think I'd like that,' said Clare.

'People to play with,' said Jack. 'Football. We could get a team.'

'Slow down,' said Mrs Roberts. 'We don't know anything of the sort, I only suggested it. It could be anything.'

'What?' demanded Jack.

'A proper house. Offices. Plenty of companies

14

are moving into the country. A nursing home.'

'Bet that's it,' said Clare.

'Huh,' Jack grunted. 'Hope it's not. No. It's a school. Betcha.'

'What do you think, Thomas?'

'I don't know. I wouldn't mind a nursing home. Or a hospital. But I'd rather it wasn't a school.'

'Dimmy,' said Jack. 'Why not?'

Thomas hesitated. 'I don't want any more children in the village. Not lots, anyway. One or two moving in would be all right. But not lots.'

'It would be great,' Jack argued.

'And they wouldn't want to play with us anyway,' said Thomas. 'Not if it was a posh school. They'd keep to themselves.'

'No. We'd show them things. The Barrow. And Parcel's Stones. And the stream and where to fish and where it isn't any good.'

'No!' said Thomas. Mrs Roberts looked at him in surprise. He was so quiet, always preferring to walk away from an argument. She liked him for being so different from her own son, who walked into trouble as soon as he saw it and quite often when he didn't see it.

'They're ours,' Thomas said fiercely. 'We can't show them to other people.'

'I'm going to,' said Jack. 'I'm going to make friends with them.'

'Well, you won't be my friend,' said Thomas. 'Not if –'

15

'You can put that crumpet down, then,' said Jack. 'If you're not my friend you can't eat my crumpets.'

'Jack!' said his mother. 'Apologise. Now.'

'Sorry,' said Jack, quickly with no conviction.

'There probably isn't going to be a school there,' said Mrs Roberts. 'And you're certainly not going to fall out over something that hasn't happened and probably won't.'

Jack looked genuinely sorry. 'Sorry,' he volunteered.

'Thomas, have another crumpet,' said Mrs Roberts. She leaned forward to hand him the dish, but it was empty.

'She's finished them,' said Jack. 'I told you. Clare's eaten the lot.'

'I'll toast some more,' said Mrs Roberts. She looked at Clare accusingly. 'For the boys.'

Clare wiped buttery fingers on her handkerchief. 'I'm full anyway,' she said.

'Five crumpets, I should think you are,' said Jack.

'What are you getting for Christmas, Thomas?' Mrs Roberts called from the kitchen.

THREE

Thomas was late home and his mother was looking out of the window for him. When she saw his small shape emerge from the darkness and the swirling snow which had begun to fall again, the worried look disappeared and she smiled. She raised her arm and waved to him through the window. Then she winced, because it still hurt to lift her arm.

Thomas waved back but he did not smile.

Sometimes he wished that she would be cross with him for being late; her relief was more uncomfortable. It seemed so mean that he had worried her and he would rather have felt naughty than mean. Not that he was very late. But it was dark so early. He thought he would mention this to make himself feel better.

'So it should be dark early,' his mother agreed. 'It's the shortest day today. Tomorrow the nights start drawing out. Soon be Christmas.'

'I saw that American woman,' said Thomas.

The house was so quiet after the noise and activity at the Robertses'. Not a sad quiet, but a gentle, comforting peacefulness. These were the best times for Thomas, when he could be on his own with his mother.

'Miss Aylmer?'

'Yes.'

'Why should she be looking at you?'

'She was.'

'You mean she was looking at the snow and you just happened to walk by.'

Thomas knew that this was wrong. He knew that the woman had been looking for him.

'The Manor is sold,' he said.

'I saw the sign. Who's that in this weather?' She peered through the window in response to a knock at the door, but the dark and the snow made seeing impossible.

Thomas had an uncomfortable feeling that it

18

was Miss Aylmer. She had looked out for him and followed him home.

'Mr Weever,' said his mother. 'Come in quickly. You'll be perished.'

'Mrs Ketch, Thomas,' the man greeted them, stepping inside. He ducked his head to avoid banging it on the not-low lintel of the door. Taking off his black cap, he banged it on his thigh, scattering snow. The cottage was very old and had no porch or hall. The living-room door opened right out on to the village green. Mr Weever dripped on the carpet as the heat from the fire melted the snow on his cloak and boots. Thomas's mother busied herself taking the long black cloak, which she handed to Thomas.

'Carry that out back, will you. You'll not mind taking your boots off, will you, Mr Weever? You'll be so much more comfortable if you do.'

'I will that,' he said. 'And your carpet will come to no harm either.' He kicked off his wellingtons and handed these over to Thomas as well. Thomas thought he had never seen such huge feet. He supposed that Mr Weever was so tall that if his feet had been any smaller they would not have been enough to keep him upright and he would have toppled over. And the boots! If I put them on, he thought, I'd be able to stride across country, like seven-league boots.

Thomas took his time hanging up the black cloak. He did not like this new vicar and he

19

resented losing his time on his own with his mother. So he lingered longer than necessary. The man's deep voice boomed out in a series of comments and laughs. Then there was a pause while Mrs Ketch spoke. Another quick laugh, then a sudden question, muffled by the door so that Thomas could not hear the words but he caught the serious tone of voice. For a while neither spoke, then Mrs Ketch said something very quietly and Thomas managed to catch his own name, nothing more, in her answer. The vicar did not laugh again, but the questions and answers carried on. When Thomas went back into the living room he found his mother putting her handkerchief away quickly. Mr Weever had his huge hand on her arm and he was looking down at her intently. He did not look away when Thomas came in and he kept his hand where it was. Thomas blushed and felt angry.

'You'll have a cup of tea, won't you?' asked Mrs Ketch.

Mr Weever shook his head. 'Not if you don't make me,' he said. 'I'm warm enough and I drink too much tea.' He took his hand away slowly but not before Thomas noticed a purple stain on his arm where it stuck out from his shirt cuff. It was a scribbled scar, like a pattern, or as though the vicar had jotted down a secret message to himself on his arm. It disappeared into the sleeve as he drew his hand away.

'Now, Thomas,' he said in a friendly way.

Thomas glared at him.

'It's carol singing next week. Around the village.'

'If you can get round,' said Thomas's mother.

'Oh, a bit of snow won't stop us. You're on, aren't you?'

'I don't know,' said Thomas.

'He'll be there,' promised his mother.

'Good. That's settled.'

'I'm not sure,' said Thomas.

'The thing is,' said the vicar, 'we need you especially. For the first verse of "Once in Royal David's City". It's a solo part.'

This annoyed Thomas even more. He wanted to sing it, especially as it made his mother look so happy. But he didn't want to sing it for Mr Weever. 'Three times might do. Four would be better, if your voice holds out. We start at eight o'clock in the Green Dragon. Just a few to get us started, then you give them your solo just before we set off round the village.'

Mrs Ketch looked hopefully at Thomas.

'All right,' he agreed.

'Just the job,' said Mr Weever. 'We couldn't manage without you.'

'Do you really think so?' said Mrs Ketch.

'I know so. You see, getting a nipper to do the solo makes them go over all funny. Really tugs the heart strings. They'll be weeping into their gin.'

Mrs Ketch looked surprised.

'Then,' said the vicar, 'as soon as they're off their guard, I go round with the collecting box. They'll have coughed up the cash before they know what's hit them.' And his laugh rang out again. 'Then it's straight round the village and end up at Viviper Cottage.'

'Where?' asked Thomas.

'Miss Felicity Aylmer's. Mulled wine, mince pies. Hot fruit punch. That's your fourth performance. I reckon if you can't sing your solo there she'll throw us out unvictualled.'

Mrs Ketch felt something of Thomas's resentment. 'Doesn't seem right, somehow. Going to a newcomer's house. She's not been here a year.'

'She offered her hospitality,' said Mr Weever. 'And she's not such a newcomer. Her links with the village go back a long time.'

'I'll be hoarse,' said Thomas.

'You can't be,' warned the vicar. 'Miss Aylmer's already told me how much she's looking forward to hearing you sing. She mentioned it particularly.'

'It'll be a wonderful Christmas,' said Mrs Ketch. 'Carols, snow already, and goodwill and peace.'

Thomas doubted it very much and allowed his face to show it. The vicar threw back his head and roared with fierce laughter, his hair wild like a lion's mane.

FOUR

The first lorry arrived at six o'clock, throwing snow to either side of its massive wheels. The next lorry ground the snow down and made it a filthy grey. The third lorry turned the snow to slush. By eight o'clock the whole village was in uproar at the convoy which went on endlessly in and out of the gates of Wivern Manor. Once through the gates, the lorries were invisible behind the great flint walls that flanked the house and gardens. As soon as each lorry was through, the gates were slammed shut.

Mr Weever stood in the porch of St Romanus' Church and watched in his cassock and cloak. Miss Aylmer watched from behind the windows of Viviper Cottage. But the rest of the village stood out in groups, huddled in overcoats and scarves against the cold.

Thomas, Jack and Clare climbed the churchyard wall to get a better look over the wall of the manor house, but it was not high enough and they saw no more than the rest of the village. Towser waded through the snow and looked up at them on the wall.

Two massive gateposts, flint with stone-dressed edges, held the iron gates in position, and perched on top of these posts were two wyverns, one either side. They reared up, threatening intruders. Their dragon's mouths gaped open, revealing sharp teeth. Their wings were outstretched, like a bird ready to fight or fly, their barbed tails curled round behind them. Their strong eagle's legs gripped the tops of the posts ready to protect the Manor.

Behind the walls the lorries ran their engines and crunched their gears. Doors were swung open and cargo was unloaded heavily and noisily into the house.

'You go and tell him,' said a woman to her neighbour. A group of people looked across to the vicar where he stood alone. There was a shuffling as people rearranged themselves but no one broke free of the group to go across to him.

'Should be doing something,' one called in a voice louder than was necessary for those who were near to him.

'New!' said a contemptuous voice, and there was a murmur of agreement.

The promptings and urgings grew more insistent until Mr Weever stepped from the porch and made his way over.

'Now then, vicar,' said Harry. 'Aren't you going to put a stop to this?'

'Well, Mr Dobbs.' The vicar smiled down at the old man. 'I don't rightly know what it is you want me to stop, or what right you think I have to stop it.'

'You're vicar, aren't you?'

'I am that.'

'Well, it's a do, all right. When the vicar can't stop folk carving up the lanes with these great doings.' Harry waved a stick at the gates as another lorry was admitted.

'As for that,' said the vicar. 'I can't see they're doing anything wrong, driving on the roads. I suppose you could say they were clearing the snow. Without them the village might be cut off.'

Although this was true, it did not make a great impression on Harry or his friends. But the rest kept silent and let him do their talking for them.

'But the noise,' Harry objected.

As Mr Weever started to reply, a tractor turned the corner, its snow plough fixed to the front. The vicar's words were lost in the roar of its engine. And when the tractor had gone, the loudest noise left was the answering roar of the vicar's laughter. 'Looks like Bob Marl's off to clear his drive,' he said. 'Now, Harry, what was that you were saying about noise?'

Harry spat into the snow in disgust.

'It's no good you being clever,' said a round-faced woman. 'It's not right. What's going on in there?'

'I've no idea,' said the vicar. 'But I suppose you could go and look, and ask, and if it's anything illegal you could report it to the police. Apart from that –' he looked round at them challengingly – 'it's none of our business.'

There was an angry chatter at this and the woman spoke out again. 'I'm not going there,' she said. 'I've no right. But you could. You're the vicar.'

'That's right,' he agreed. 'I am. And in time I'll visit, to welcome them to the village. And I won't forget that they're just as much my parish as you are. I'll bid you good morning.' His broad smile of farewell was not returned by any of the people and Harry spat again loudly as he went.

Mr Weever knocked on the door of Viviper Cottage and was admitted so swiftly that it was

26

obvious that Felicity Aylmer had been watching him and was ready to open the door as soon as he arrived.

'I don't like him,' said Thomas as the three children watched him disappear. They had not been able to hear any of the conversation but the faces made it clear what had been happening and that Thomas was not alone in not liking the new vicar.

'You're his pet, though,' said Clare.

Jack made a strangled noise that was meant to be Thomas singing but sounded more like a crow with a stomachache.

Thomas pushed him off the wall, then dropped down himself. Clare followed. They trudged out of the churchyard and across the field next to it.

The snow had made the countryside a foreign place for them. Ditches and ridges had disappeared; familiar hedges were no more than white slopes where the snow had drifted against them. Trees, bare and black just two days ago, now hung white above them with a brilliant harvest.

They reached the large mound that marked the border of Herpeton, their village, and the next, Barrowdale. The mound was a rounded earthwork, higher than the church, which had not been built until at least a thousand years later. Nearby was a group of prehistoric standing stones in a circle – Parcel's Stones, they were called locally, though there was no record of who

27

or what Parcel was, or what it meant. Long ago, before any books were written in that place or houses built that still stood, half-naked tribes had gathered thousands and thousands of loads of earth and had built it up into this mound, this barrow. There was a story that right in the centre there was a king buried in a wooden ship. It was said that if you dug into the heart of the mound you would find his bones hidden in the rotted timbers, and you would see the gold jewellery that he still wore in death as he had in life, the ornaments of a monarch.

A team of experts had dug a few trenches about twenty years earlier and had found nothing. They decided that perhaps the Barrow had been a fortification, not a grave, or that it had been a grave and had been robbed not long after the king was buried, or that it had been built for pagan worship. They were not sure, but they said that there was definitely no king there now, no treasure. Jack, Clare and Thomas knew all about what the experts said, but they did not believe it. They knew that a king slept beneath the mound. They often played on the Barrow, but not in the stone circle, which they found unpleasant and unwelcoming.

But now they were not interested in the king so much as in the mound and the snow that lay on it.

'It's perfect,' said Thomas.

'But we can't,' said Clare. 'We haven't got one.'

'A tray would do,' said Jack.

'Do you think?' wondered Thomas.

'Should think so,' Jack said. 'It's just like a sledge.'

'Let's try,' said Clare.

'Home, Towser,' called Jack.

Towser left off digging a hole in the snow on the side of the Barrow and yelped his way down to the invisible path which the children had followed by habit, although it was now hidden by the snow. He ran far ahead of them, as he often did, and was soon gone.

Mr Weever was back in the churchyard when they crossed it. He waved.

'I hope you'll both be there to support Thomas at the carol singing,' he said.

'Yes,' said Clare.

'I might,' said Jack.

'I hope so,' he said warmly. 'We would love your company, even if your voice would not be missed.'

Jack scowled.

'Perhaps you would like to pass the collecting box round?' suggested Mr Weever. 'They give more to an innocent face.'

Jack knew that Mr Weever was somehow being rude to him, but he was sure that this did not give him permission to be rude back. Lots of grown-ups took advantage like that. When they were rude it was a joke. When you were rude back it was just rude.

'I'll sing, I think,' he said. 'Help Thomas along.'

They sped out through the gate towards home.

'You won't, will you?' said Thomas anxiously.

'What?'

'Sing. You won't sing.'

'I might,' threatened Jack. Jack had been pulled out of class on his first week in the infants'.

'We've got a growler,' said Miss Markworthy. 'Can't have a growler.'

And he had not sung since.

'Where's Towser?' asked Clare. Towser should have been sitting on the step laughing at them when they arrived at the house, but there was no sign of him.

'Inside already,' said Jack. 'Eating.'

But Mrs Roberts had not let him in, nor seen him.

'He'll be back at the Barrow,' predicted Jack.

Clare checked that he wasn't around. She stood on the step and whistled. Thomas looked at her in envy. She put two fingers in her mouth and blew and the most wonderful noise shrilled out.

She grinned at him. 'Sorry,' she said.

Last summer Clare had tried for two weeks to teach Thomas to whistle like that. He wanted to so much. But it was no good.

'No one taught me,' she said at last. 'I just did it. I suppose you either can or you can't.'

Thomas agreed, but he still practised sometimes when he was on his own.

The whistling did not produce Towser.

The few people who were still standing around glared at Clare. Most had gone. The lorries had unloaded and disappeared, making more slush and spraying it on the sides of the houses nearest the road. All was quiet for the moment.

The trays made passable sledges, but they were too light to pack the snow down into a proper surface and too small to ride for more than a short distance. So, although it was fun trying, they all agreed that it was not the real thing and they gave up. Towser had not been waiting for them either at the Barrow or at Jack and Clare's house when they returned for the second time.

Thomas ran home in time for lunch and burst into the cottage.

'Mum, Towser's missing. He's really gone. We'll have to go looking for him this afternoon. He's got lost in the snow.'

But his mother was not there and the look on his father's face told Thomas that there was more to worry about than a missing dog.

FIVE

Felicity Aylmer handed the vicar a glass of whisky and hot water.

'They're in a state,' she said. Her voice was harsh, unmusical, not at all like the sort of pleasant drawl the locals had expected when they heard that an American woman was coming to the village.

'New England,' she explained when she first saw their puzzled faces. 'Woods and water – lakes

and hills. And we speak up and we speak clearly.'
She only needed to say it in a loud voice once in
the post office and all the village knew. It saved
a lot of time. The other way to get something
known around the village was to tell Mr
Symondson in secret. Mr Symondson, who had
been looking for work for seventeen years now
without finding anything, had a special way with
secrets; he thought that it meant you had to tell
everyone, but only one at a time, and tell them
it was a secret. Miss Aylmer had only to walk
out of her door to his bench on the village green
and whisper a secret into his ear and within
forty-eight hours everyone in the village knew
it. She could watch him beckon them over one
by one and buzz the words discreetly in their
ears. The snow meant that he now traded his
secrets in the Green Dragon over one half-pint
of beer which he could make last for two hours,
unless someone bought him another. Although
he was out of Miss Aylmer's sight, she knew he
was still there if she needed him. He was a
reliable bass in the small choir at the church.

'Splendid,' said Mr Weever, sipping the hot
toddy.

'What?' she asked. 'Splendid that they're in a
state?'

Mr Weever laughed. 'Splendid whisky,' he
said. 'Just the thing to warm you up. But I don't
argue that it's splendid about the village. I like

33

to see them in a state. It suits our purposes very well.'

A jewelled rope slid over his arm.

'All right, Shakti,' he said. 'Have a try.' And he held out his glass to the snake, but it only sniffed once and then turned away.

'Careful,' warned Miss Aylmer.

The vicar watched the snake slip from his black robe. 'He won't touch me,' he said.

'Don't you be so sure,' Miss Aylmer said with a little smile. 'He's due to be milked. One small bite now and you'd be dead in ten minutes.'

Mr Weever pushed back the cuff of his cassock and revealed the full design of the tattoo that Thomas had glimpsed the other night. It was a purple snake writhing up the vicar's arm, mouth yawning, fangs revealed, with a drop of venom spilling out and trickling down to his wrist.

'I think I'm safe enough,' he claimed.

'I wouldn't be so sure,' she said. 'Shakti's a foreign snake. That thing of yours might work against the local vipers, but I wouldn't bet on it against an Indian cobra.'

Shakti reared up and spread his hood, swaying his head from side to side and staring at Mr Weever's arm.

'See,' she said.

'He's playing,' said the vicar confidently. 'And, anyway, there's the book.'

Miss Aylmer looked at him with wide eyes.

'You've got Thomas Kych's book?'

Mr Weever dug into the pocket of his cassock and brought out a small book, the size of the palm of a small hand. It was bound in dark leather. Felicity Aylmer put out her hand for it.

'Is it really?'

She turned it over. There was a small wyvern indented on the front cover. It had once been gilt, but all the gold had rubbed away save for a few grains, which glowed at her.

She opened it. The pages were thick and yellow. The writing – not printing – was still black, in a neat, regular hand. It was a notebook. Small pictures and diagrams illustrated the text, all hand-drawn.

'It is,' she said.

Mr Weever shook his head. 'Not really.'

'No?'

'It's Thomas Kych's all right. But not the book we want. It's just recipes, ideas, thoughts. It isn't the real book.'

'Where did you get it?'

'County Archives. All the old church records are there. It was in a shoebox with all sorts of other stuff.'

Miss Aylmer looked interested.

'No,' he said. 'Just junk. I checked it all.'

'Did you have trouble getting them to give it to you?'

'It's mine,' he said. 'I'm the vicar.'

'Did you have to sign for it?'

Mr Weever smiled. 'It seemed a waste of time bothering them with paperwork. It seemed easier just to slip it into my pocket.'

'Anyone could have found it and taken it,' she said.

Mr Weever nodded solemnly. 'We're just in time.'

'And the real book? Perhaps they've already got it.'

'No. They would have taken this as well. We're still ahead of them. Just.'

'Perhaps it's in the Manor? Perhaps they've got it.'

'I don't think so. But we'll soon know.'

Shakti hissed. He slid down Weever's arm, across the snake tattoo.

'Better be careful,' said Miss Aylmer.

She took a glass from a small cabinet, stretched a clean handkerchief tightly over it and picked up Shakti. She stroked his neck, waited for him to open his mouth and then fastened his teeth into the membrane of linen over the mouth of the glass. Cobra kissed tumbler and drops of venom dripped into the glass. Shakti bit and bit again until all his poison had dribbled away. Then Miss Aylmer put him down gently and stroked him.

'There's a snake,' she said. 'There's a good snake.' She took the glass away into another room.

'They'll be in even more of a state when they find out what's really happening at the Manor,' he predicted.

Miss Aylmer agreed. 'But that will take some time,' she said.

'Oh, I don't know,' he said. 'I might just wander down the Dragon. Have a quiet word with Mr Symondson.'

'In confidence,' said Felicity Aylmer.

'Oh, yes. In confidence. I can't be seen gossiping to the whole village.'

'That should do it,' she said.

'Probably only take a day. News like this,' he said.

They raised their glasses, toasted one another and drank the hot whisky.

The roads were still difficult to drive on outside the village. The lorries had churned the snow up, but the fresh falls overnight had filled the gaps and the going was difficult. Thomas's father gripped the wheel tight in his large hands, scarred and rough from the work he did on Bob Marl's farm. But it was not just the effort of driving in the bad snow that made him grip so tight, it was worry about Thomas and fear of the future.

'She's fine,' he had told Thomas at bedtime. 'We'll see her tomorrow.'

'She's not fine,' he argued. 'They don't take you to hospital if you're fine, do they?'

37

His father ignored the belligerent tone of the question and answered him softly. Like many powerful men, Ted Ketch was gentle and he hated to hurt anything. 'Of course she's not fine,' he said, 'I didn't mean it like that. I mean, she'll get well again, and the best place for her to do that is in hospital.'

Even Thomas could not argue with that. He knew he would not sleep all night and lay with his eyes wide open against the darkness. He heard his father boil a kettle for a hot drink, heard him wash up the cup, and then he heard him going downstairs to boil the kettle again for his breakfast. The night had gone.

But even the morning did not make anything feel better. And the snow, which had been such a treat and an adventure yesterday, was now a nuisance slowing down their trip to the hospital.

Mrs Ketch smiled very brightly at them from her high bed.

Thomas slipped his hand into hers and hoped that no one was looking when he kissed her.

'It was just a little sudden,' she explained. 'A bit of pain that told me the operation hadn't sorted everything out properly. But they'll get it this time. And I won't be here long.'

Ted Ketch sat silently at the foot of the bed while his wife and son talked. He did not interfere until they fell into a silence which Thomas found more difficult than the evasive answers to his worried questions. Then Ted put his hand in his pocket and pulled out some money. 'There's a shop downstairs,' he said. 'Buy your mother some peppermints, will you?' Thomas took the money. 'And get something for yourself.'

When he returned he was surprised to see that his mother was holding his father and comforting him. His father's eyes were red but his mother was smiling. It was all the wrong way round somehow.

'I won't sing the carols now,' said Thomas. He had made up his mind.

'But you must.'

'Not if you're not there to hear them. I was only doing it for you.'

'Well, do it for me still, please.'

'I don't know. Not if you can't hear them.'

'We'll see about it later,' said his father. 'Don't go upsetting your mother.'

That was when Thomas began to cry, although he had promised himself he wouldn't.

The sign over the pub door swung in the wind so that the green dragon painted on it swayed and moved as if alive. Mr Weever passed under the notice that read: *L. S. Caton, licensed to sell retail beer, wines and spirits for consumption on or off the premises.*

L. S. Caton himself was not there. He was hardly ever there. He ran the pub as a hobby

39

and for a small profit, having enough money of his own not to need to work. At the moment he was in Switzerland on a skiing holiday. The locals had been delighted to read reports in the newspapers that Switzerland was having the warmest winter in memory and the ski slopes were green and wet.

'Could have stayed here,' they jeered, 'and skied down the Barrow.'

This always brought a gale of laughter.

The genial buzz of talk dropped to a whisper when Mr Weever stepped in. New vicars are always treated with suspicion and Mr Weever was not liked.

But he ignored the hostile silence and bought himself another whisky. 'And a pint for you, Mr Symondson?' he called over.

'Oh, aye, if you like, vicar,' he said.

'And if you've got a minute I wouldn't mind a few words about the carol singing.'

Mr Symondson detached himself from the group and joined the vicar at a corner table.

Mr Weever leaned forward. 'It's not really about the choir at all,' he said. 'But I wanted your advice, as a long resident of the village. It's about what they're going to be doing with the manor house.'

'Oh, aye,' said Mr Symondson.

'Well,' said the vicar. 'In confidence, of course . . .'

SIX

'Where've you been?' demanded Jack. 'We've been looking for you all morning. You weren't there and we needed you,' he accused Thomas.

Clare noticed how pale Thomas was behind his freckles.

'Are you ill?' she asked.

"Course he's not ill,' said Jack. 'You can see that. He's not in bed, is he?'

'What's up?' asked Thomas.

'It's Towser,' said Jack. 'He's gone.'

Clare looked at Thomas.

'Are you sure you're all right?'

'Is he really missing?' asked Thomas.

'Yes,' she said.

'Since yesterday. Call yourself a friend! You were there when he went missing.'

'I thought he'd turn up,' said Thomas. 'Dogs often go off for a bit on their own.'

'Well, he hasn't,' said Jack. 'Turned up, that is. We've been looking all morning. Where were you?'

'Did you try the Barrow?'

'First place we looked.'

'And round by the cow sheds at Bob Marl's?'

'Yes.'

'What about down at the brook?'

'Why?'

'We often go there with him. He might have gone looking for us and fallen in.'

'Come on,' shouted Jack, and he set off running. Thomas followed, but Clare caught up with him quickly.

'What's up?' she asked.

'Find Towser first,' he said. It was difficult to speak while they were running through the snow.

The brook was frozen over.

'Let's slide on it,' said Jack, forgetting about Towser.

'Don't be stupid,' said Clare. 'You'll fall through and drown.'

Jack tried his foot on the edge of the ice and it creaked.

'Might hold me,' he said.

'No,' said Clare. 'I'm going home if you try.'

'Don't,' said Thomas.

'Frightened?' said Jack.

'No,' he said. 'But I don't think you should break the ice. Not yet.'

'Why?'

'We want to see if there's a hole that Towser might have fallen through.'

Jack looked suitably ashamed.

'Right,' he agreed. 'We'll walk along the edge.'

At first there was no break in the ice. When Jack saw the first hole he yelled, 'He's in there!'

'Where?' said Clare.

Jack pointed.

'It's a hole,' said Thomas. 'But I don't think it's big enough for Towser to have fallen through.'

Then there were more holes and more, and bigger ones.

'Look,' said Clare. She showed them a large stone on the ice that had cracked the surface but not broken through. 'It's people playing,' she said. 'Smashing the ice with rocks.'

'So it's not Towser,' said Jack with relief.

'Could be,' said Thomas.

'What?'

43

'Just because some of the holes aren't Towser, doesn't mean none of them are, is, I think.'

Jack barged into Thomas with his shoulder.

'You're no help,' he said. 'You're just making us upset.'

'I'll go then,' offered Thomas, and he turned to leave.

'And you weren't there when we wanted you. Remember that!' Jack called after him. 'Where are you going, Clare?'

'Stupid!' she said.

'It's all right,' said Thomas.

'What's happened?'

Thomas turned and saw that Jack had stayed by the brook and was throwing stones on to the ice.

'It's Mum,' he said. 'She's back in hospital.' And he told her.

It took less than twenty-four hours for Mr Symondson to get the news round the village.

Within seven hours there was a meeting in the Church Hall. Mr Weever refused to act as chair but he was there. So was Miss Aylmer. Thomas and Jack and Clare were not supposed to be but they perched on a window-sill at the back and no one bothered to throw them out.

Bob Marl was persuaded to chair the meeting.

'It ought to be the vicar,' he protested.

'It ought to be someone from the Manor, come

to that,' said Mr Weever. 'I suppose the new owner is the squire now.'

People complained loudly at the bad taste of his remark.

'It can hardly be someone from the Manor,' pointed out Bob Marl, 'when this meeting's supposed to be getting rid of them.'

'Popular vote, then,' said the vicar. 'Looks like it's you.'

Thomas waited for the great laugh to burst out but the vicar contented himself with a silent smile.

Miss Aylmer, who was sitting next to him, fumbled in her coat as though she had fleas.

The meeting eventually managed to start and Bob Marl called for order.

'It seems,' he said, 'that the Manor is being turned into a laboratory or something of the kind.'

All eyes turned to Mr Symondson. He was clearly unwilling to break his habit and speak to a group of people, but the pressure forced him to his feet.

'A place for experimenting on animals,' he said. 'That's all I know.'

'What sort of experiments?'

'Is it for farming, or medicine?'

'It's for cosmetics. I know it's cosmetics.'

'Shame!'

'Beagles. They use beagles. They make them

45

smoke cigarettes.'

'And rabbits. They drop things in their eyes.'

'I suppose it could be useful. Medical research.'

'Boo!'

'It has to happen. It saves lives.'

'Shame!'

Mr Symondson sat down.

Bob Marl banged an ashtray on the table. 'Order. Order! Will you come to order, please?'

'Poor creatures.'

'Order!'

'We'll have to – '

'Order. Silence!' he bellowed.

The hall fell silent.

'Can't you take over, vicar?' he begged. 'I'm no good at this.'

'You seem to be doing very well,' the vicar encouraged him. 'Go on.'

Old Harry Dobbs stood up. 'It's all right well,' he said, 'all this talk. But what do we know? Nothing. Who tells us? No one. I'm off to the Dragon.'

'Don't go,' someone called.

'You can tell me later, maybe. If you know anything to tell.'

'Harry's right,' said Bob. 'We don't know anything. How do you know, Mr Symondson?'

Everyone ignored Mr Symondson and looked at the vicar. They all knew he had talked to him in the Green Dragon at lunchtime.

'He told me,' said Mr Symondson. 'Vicar.'

Well?' asked Bob.

'I discussed the carols with you in the Green Dragon,' said Mr Weever. 'Isn't that right?'

'It is,' said Mr Symondson. 'And other things.'

'Were these other things confidential?' asked the vicar.

'They were.'

'Then I have no wish to discuss them further,' he said. 'And I'm sure you would wish to keep silent, too, whatever they were about.'

'Was it about the Manor?' asked Bob.

'It was confidential,' said the vicar. 'I'm afraid I could not betray a trust by talking about it in public.'

There was an angry buzz from the crowd. Mr Weever smiled at them, unconcerned.

'This won't do, vicar,' said Mrs Reeves. 'You'll have to say. It's your duty, you know. And, I might add, you've not been in the village long and you're making a very bad start.'

Mrs Reeves was a podgy woman with a squashed face who had only lived in the village a few years and who acted as though she had ancestors in the churchyard going back centuries.

'Of course, Mrs Reeves, if you would like to release me from my obligations to keep secrets I will be happy to do so. Now, where shall I start? There was the affair of the fence, I think, that was repaired in a different place and gave extra land – '

'Vicar!' said Mrs Reeves. 'I'm shocked. You can't talk about that.'

'It was in confidence?' he asked.

'Strictest confidence.'

He smiled and sat back. 'It seems I am forbidden to speak,' he said. 'But if I might make a suggestion?'

'Anything,' said Bob Marl.

'We could invite the new owner of the Manor to come to a meeting and discuss his plans with us.'

Bob Marl quickly managed to get this agreed and the meeting was dissolved.

'You'll take the message to them, won't you?' he asked as people left.

'Gladly. Give me a written copy and I'll take it round.' He smiled at the three children on the window-sill and followed the others out.

'He's in with them,' said Jack.

'Who?' asked Thomas.

'The new people at the Manor. He told old Symondson. Everyone knew that.'

They climbed down.

'I'm really sorry about your mum,' Jack said.

Thomas nodded. 'It's all right.'

'I was a pig,' he said.

'No, you – '

'Yes, he was,' said Clare.

Thomas smiled. 'All right,' he said. 'He was a

pig. But it's all right.'

'Here,' Jack complained. 'I was only being polite. I wasn't really a pig.'

'Yes, you were,' said Clare. 'If you think I'm going to let you – '

Jack interrupted. 'Towser!' he said.

'Where?' Thomas looked round.

'They've taken him into the Manor. You heard. Experiments on animals. They've taken Towser.'

They ran out of the hall and stared at the Manor. The wyverns lifted their heads into the night sky in threatening laughter.

'We'll never get him out,' wailed Clare.

'Oh, yes, we will,' promised Jack. 'Listen. This is what we'll do.'

SEVEN

Towser was barking. Thomas heard him. It was half a bark and half a howl, as though he was hurt or trapped. Thomas looked round for him in the darkness but there was no sign of him, just the barking. Thomas climbed the wall of the churchyard and leaped over the flint wall of the Manor as though it were a low fence. The two wyverns on the gateposts turned their heads and watched him land safely on the other side.

Towser kept on barking. They flexed their wings. Thomas darted into a dark corner but he knew that their eyes could burn through the night and see him in the gloomiest place. And all the time Towser barked pitifully, begging him to help.

Thomas skirted round the house until he found a window half open. He lifted it a little more, then put his leg over the sill to climb in. As soon as he began to enter the house the wyverns threw back their heads, let out wild howls of delight and leaped from their gateposts. They cut through the air and plunged down towards Thomas, shrieking in attack. Thomas pushed himself through the window and into the house. He jumped clear. There was no floor inside and he started to fall. His stomach rushed to meet his throat.

Towser barked for help. The wyverns swooped down to harry him.

Thomas threw out his arms to break his fall and jerked out of sleep. His bedclothes were tied around him, wet with the sweat of fear. His heart was racing. He lay back and waited for the room to steady itself and for his relief at being safe in bed to overwhelm him.

But Towser was still barking for help. Thomas rose unsteadily and looked out of his window.

The wyverns turned to look at him from their gateposts. He closed his eyes and looked again. He called himself a fool. They had not turned at all, they still looked inwards to each other, but that meant that one always looked towards his window, as it did now, while the other looked away.

Thomas listened. Towser suddenly stopped barking. The snow was falling again. There was a single light in the manor house, high up. All else was dark and still and silent.

A wave of relief swept over Thomas. It was all a dream. It had not been Towser. He had still been half asleep. Everything was fine.

Suddenly, his stomach rushed to meet his throat again. Mum wasn't there. She was in hospital, still not well, even after the operation. They still had to do things to make her better. A machine, she said. Some kind of rays or something. He didn't understand. He stumbled to the bathroom and threw up in the lavatory bowl.

A light went on on the landing.

His father waited until he was finished and then led him back to his room. He had no words. Ted Ketch had never been too good at words, but he sat on Thomas's bed and sang softly until he was asleep again, and for a long time afterwards.

Jane Gwyer looked calmly at the riot going on around and below her.

The board saying ACQUIRED FOR CLIENTS had been changed to read:

ACQUIRED FOR ~~CLIENTS~~
MURDERERS

A lorry revved its engine threateningly at the crowd blocking the gate.

Overnight the village had sat up making placards and posters:

ANIMALS HAVE RIGHTS, TOO
STOP THIS TORTURE
DEATH-CAMP MANOR
FREE THE VICTIMS
HERPETON SAYS NO!
LIVES, NOT LIPSTICKS

The way up to the gates was blocked with people waving the banners and chanting: 'Killers – out! Killers. Killers. Killers. Out! Out! Out!'

The driver put his foot hard on the accelerator and the engine roared. A few people stood aside, but Harry Dobbs stood firm and shook his fist. The lorry inched forward but Harry would not move. The driver put the brake on and let his head fall into his hands.

'Turn back,' someone urged him. 'They're murdering animals.'

He lifted his hands in resignation but did not turn away.

Two men stood in the gateway, waiting to swing the iron gates open if the crowd parted.

53

'Drive through 'em,' one of the men called to the driver. He beckoned him forward. The driver revved the engine again, but the crowd stood firm.

Something began to howl. The villagers hushed and listened.

'In the lorry,' said one. 'Dogs.'

They banged on the sides of the lorry and their blows were answered with a yapping and a howling.

'Killers!' screamed one of the younger men who had recently come to the village.

'Let them out,' his wife called.

They struggled ineffectually with the doors of the lorry.

'No good. We can't push them open. Turn him over.'

The crowd rushed round to one side and started to rock the vehicle. The driver had been patiently helpless until then, but now he saw the danger and he saw his chance. Most of the people were on one side so he slipped quickly into gear, darted forward and leaned on the horn. The few who were left at the front saw that he was serious. Only Old Harry stood his ground and if Mr Weever had not pulled him away at the last moment he would have fallen beneath the wheels of the lorry.

The gates swung open and the lorry was in. The newcomer who had tried to open the lorry doors tried to follow it in. He was pushed roughly away by one of the guards and fell into the muddy snow, his nose bleeding.

Before the gate could be swung shut, Mr Weever stepped inside. The guards looked startled and did not challenge him. Whether it was the authority of the cassock or the threat of his great height and size was never clear to anyone watching.

'I have a letter for your employer,' he said to the first guard. And he held up a white envelope.

'I'll take it,' said the guard.

Mr Weever snatched it away. 'No,' he said. 'I'll deliver it myself. I'm coming to welcome him to the parish, and I need to do that personally.'

The guards were reluctant to let him in.

'This way, I imagine,' he said, and strode off to the front door before they could stop him.

There was a small cheer.

'He's through,' said someone.

'He let the lorry through,' said Harry.

'And he's maybe not on our side,' said Harry's friend.

'He'll not help,' said Mrs Reeves. 'Mark my words. He'll butter them up, all right. He won't help us. He's new. He doesn't understand the village.'

Harry's friend led him away before he could remind Mrs Reeves of how long she had lived in Herpeton.

A few placards stayed and waved threateningly at the rest of the lorries as they drove up during the morning. There was no more chanting and no one tried seriously to prevent them from entering. The vicar stayed a long time.

'We'll never get in there,' said Thomas. 'Not with all those guards.'

Jack led them round the wall and into the field behind the Manor. There was a round brick building huddled against the flint wall. 'The ice house,' said Jack. 'They used to store ice here in the old days and it kept all through the summer. We can climb up it and over the wall.'

'We're not allowed here,' said Clare. 'It belongs to the Manor.'

'Doesn't matter,' said Jack. 'They're only bothered about the front.'

Thomas looked doubtful. 'They'll watch this as well,' he said.

'Later,' said Jack. 'When they're settled. They'll patrol it then. Right now, all they're bothered about is the gates. With all those people there. They can't watch everywhere. We'll come back when it's dark, and slip in. Then we can find Towser.'

'He isn't in there,' said Clare.

'Then we'll know that when we've looked,' said Jack. 'Are you on?' he asked Thomas.

Thomas nodded.

'I heard Towser last night,' he said. 'At least,

I think I did. It woke me up.'

'See,' said Jack. 'He's trapped. Are you in, too, Clare?'

Clare looked at the ice house. She could see that even from its roof they would never be able to scale the wall. It was just too high. 'All right,' she said, knowing that it was safe to say it. 'I'll come.'

'Great,' said Jack.

They carried on past the walls of the Manor and to the Barrow. Clare hoped that Towser would be there. She hated the thought of some-one trapping him. She wanted him back without any fuss.

They built a snow fort and pelted each other. It was strong and high and one person could easily defend it against the other two.

They were wet and tired when they trudged home. Mr Weever did not see them as he opened the side gate of the Manor, the one that led directly into the churchyard. He locked it behind him and went into the church.

'He's got a key,' said Jack. 'Did you see? He's got a key.'

They agreed. They had seen.

'He's in with them. I knew he was,' said Jack. 'He's stolen Towser.'

'Come on,' said Clare. 'That's silly.'

'We can take the key,' said Thomas. 'We don't need the ice house.'

'What?' asked Clare.

'He hangs all the keys up in a cupboard in the church. I've watched him.'

Jack hugged Thomas. Clare hugged herself with worry.

Mr Weever came back out of the church and saw them.

'Hi,' he called. 'I want a word.'

EIGHT

The hospital ward was warm and busy. Nurses moved from bed to bed chatting to patients, straightening sheets, giving medicine, pouring drinks, shaking pillows, smiling at cheerful ones, giving a hug or a quiet word to lonely and frightened ones. Outside, white flakes of snow battered against the windows, soft against the black sky.

The small buzz of activity fell to a silence as a clear voice from nowhere broke through the evening: 'Once in royal David's city . . .'

Mrs Ketch put down her book and looked up. The ward doors swung open and a robed procession entered, in twos, with Thomas on his own at the back singing the first verse of the hymn. When he had finished the others joined in, first in unison, then, as the song drew on, breaking into harmony and coming together again at the end with a full-throated unison conclusion.

Thomas's mother gripped the sheets and lay quite still. She made no attempt to stop the tears that flowed down her cheeks, or to wipe them away until the music was quite over. Then she hurriedly applied her handkerchief before Thomas could look up at her. They sang several more carols before they finished and she was quite in control by the time Thomas came over. His face was lit with joy.

'Did you like it?' he asked.

She began to cry again when she tried to answer, and this made Thomas cry as well. The rest of the choir walked around the ward chatting to patients and offering them mince pies. Mr Weever kept away from Thomas and his mother until they were both wiped dry of tears and Mrs Ketch called him over.

'Thank you *so* much,' she said. She gripped his hand. 'Thank you.'

'Couldn't stay away,' he said. 'Not after you'd given us Thomas to sing.'

Thomas scowled. He wished the vicar would leave them alone. When he had called them over to him in the churchyard the day before, Thomas and the others thought they were in trouble. Thomas still thought it was a mean trick of the vicar's. He, Thomas, had intended to give up the carol singing. He didn't want to, not with Mum in hospital, and he didn't want to go to Miss Aylmer's afterwards. But when the vicar had suggested going to the hospital first, there was no way out of doing the whole thing.

'Have to go soon, though,' said Mr Weever. 'We're due at the Dragon at eight o'clock.' He looked at his watch and, as his cuff fell away, Thomas saw for the first time what the pattern on the vicar's arm was. He shuddered. The snake seemed to be alive in the movement of the man's broad arm.

The dragon seemed to be alive in the rippling of the banner as it caught the night wind. It was a two-legged dragon with wings and a gaping mouth. Cruel talons grasped for prey. Above its head was written '*St Romanus' Church*' and beneath its feet '*Herpeton*'. The dragon and the words were embroidered in silk threads on a silk background.

'We've never carried the banner round the village before, vicar,' grumbled Old Harry.

'Shame,' said Mr Weever. 'Hold it steady, Jack.

61

Good to give the old boy an outing. You never know. It must get lonely in there. It'll be pleased to see its relatives.'

'Eh?' grunted Harry.

The vicar pointed to the wyverns on the gate-posts of the Manor.

'They must be related,' he said.

Harry looked puzzled, then annoyed. Mr Weever threw back his head and laughed.

'To the Green Dragon,' he ordered. 'Another relation, no doubt.'

The choir processed across the snow-covered green, beneath the steady smile of Miss Jane Gwyer and up to the door of the pub. Clare looked at the banner as it swayed in the wind beneath the pub sign. She had never noticed before, but the vicar was right; the two dragons were related. They each had two legs and the same wings and wide mouths; the same, in fact, she realised, as the wyverns on the gateposts of Wivern Manor. And she looked across and saw the two wyverns, black shapes against a bright sky dusted with stars.

'Ready?' said Mr Weever. 'One, two.'

The choir broke into song and he swung open the pub door.

There were one or two scowls among the welcoming smiles in the bar, from customers who didn't like to have their drinking interrupted or maybe feared that they would have to dig deep for the collection. But the power of the music broke down all resistance and, by the time Thomas opened his solo, several people, men as well as women, were looking for their handkerchiefs. When the vicar produced his collecting bag, the money flowed generously.

The night was mild and the snow crunched pleasantly underfoot as the choir trailed round the village, the two lines of robed figures snaking round corners and up slopes like a dragon. Doors opened and people stood on their steps in slippers and listened to the singers. Thomas sang once more but Mr Weever told him not to bother with another solo, to wait until they reached Viviper Cottage. Not that they needed any more hospitality. Mince pies, drinks, biscuits and chocolates were offered wherever they sang. Clare noticed that Mr Symondson never refused a drink, whether it were wine, sherry or beer. To her surprise, the vicar also took a drink at every stop. But while Mr Symondson was beginning to look a little unsteady on his feet, the vicar seemed not to be affected by it at all.

All too soon for Thomas, the trip round the village was over and they were back at the village green outside Viviper Cottage. They formed up and he started his solo again. Doors opened and smiling faces looked out. But Viviper Cottage remained shut. His hopes rose as he began to think that Miss Aylmer had changed her mind, or gone out. They sang three carols and collected more money and drinks. As the last notes faded away, Miss Aylmer opened her door and welcomed them.

'I like to hear it all from behind the door,' she said. 'As though you were unseen angels.'

'Yuk,' said Jack to Clare.

Clare grinned.

Thomas bit the corner of his hymn book.

'Welcome,' said Miss Aylmer. 'Clovis, bring your angels in.'

Clare mouthed silently at Thomas: *Clovis?*

The dragon banner shook in Jack's hands as he stifled a laugh.

'You'll need to lower that,' said Mr Weever. He took the banner and lifted the image from the pole.

The cottage seemed bigger inside than it ought to be but it was still quite a squash getting everyone inside. The mulled wine hung a veil of spices in the air. Miss Aylmer gave Clare a plate of mince pies.

'Would you give these out, please,' she said in her harsh foreign voice, 'while I pour the wine?'

Clare took the plate. 'One for you, angel,' she whispered to Thomas.

Thomas spluttered.

Miss Aylmer broke her walk and came back to Clare. She gave her a broad smile which frightened Clare more than an angry look could have done.

'There are also fallen angels,' she said. 'Devils. Dragons. The wicked serpent.'

Thomas arrested the mince pie in his mouth in half-bite. Jack held his halfway up to his mouth. Miss Aylmer smiled again and turned away to pour her drinks.

'Wow,' said Thomas, when he was quite sure that he could not be heard.

As usual, the grown-ups were getting on with their own conversations and ignoring the three children, for which they were very grateful. Harry, his face red with drink and the night air, started a chorus of 'While Shepherds Watched' to the tune of 'On Ilkley Moor Ba'at 'at' and the others joined in.

Miss Aylmer brought three glasses of hot fruit punch over. They thanked her politely and looked at it suspiciously.

'It's all right,' she assured them. 'No alcohol. I don't want your parents coming round to complain. Oh, and Thomas, I'm very sorry to hear about your mother.'

Thomas nodded. He did not want to discuss his mother with this woman.

'Perhaps you can come round tomorrow morning,' she said. 'I've got something I'd like to give you for her.'

'I'll take it tonight,' he said. 'Save you trouble.'

Miss Aylmer smiled. 'No. No, I haven't

wrapped it yet. Tomorrow morning would be better, if you can make it.'

Jack and Clare looked at Thomas. He was prepared to be rude enough to refuse but he couldn't bear to be thought afraid.

'Ten o'clock?' he asked casually.

'That's fine,' she agreed. 'I'll have it ready.'

NINE

At three o'clock in the morning the doors and
windows of the village opened again. But not to
hear the carol singers.

Terrible yelps and howling and baying broke
through the night. The moon swung over the
Manor and looked down on the open windows of
the cottages.

The noise lasted for a minute at the most, but
it was so deathly, so frightening that it seemed

much longer.

Thomas's father sat with him in the window and looked out.

'It's a bad business,' he said when the barking had stopped.

'Yes.'

'But she'll be all right.'

'Will she?'

'They shouldn't be doing it to those animals,' he said.

'It's not right,' agreed Thomas.

'She was glad you went tonight,' said his father. 'She was glad she heard you sing.'

Thomas slipped his hand into his father's rough hand. They sat in silence.

'What are they doing to those animals?' he asked at length.

'Experiments.'

'What for?'

'Don't know. They do all sorts these days.'

Thomas thought. 'Is it for medicine?'

'Sometimes.'

'Will it make Mum better?'

Mr Ketch could not answer.

'I mean,' said Thomas, 'if they could make Mum better by experimenting on the dogs and other animals, wouldn't that be worth it?'

'You heard them,' said his father. 'Just then. You heard them.'

He put Thomas to bed, kissed him and

went out.

Thomas waited until all was still, then went back to the window. He looked at the houses round the green. The lights were off now and everyone back in bed. He shivered a little. He was not tired at all. He remembered Mum in the hospital bed, her hands gripping the sheet when he was singing.

Something moved outside.

Thomas leaned forward.

A small noise of crunching snow. A creak. A lock snapping shut. Thomas scanned the green. He looked at the gates of the Manor. He looked at the churchyard.

A huge figure swathed in a black cloak stepped from the shadows of the wall. It crossed the graveyard, through the gate, over the green. When it reached Viviper Cottage the door opened and it went in.

Thomas looked at his clock; half past three.

He waited to see the figure come back out. At half past four he woke up, cold and stiff in the window. He dragged himself back to bed and was in a very bad mood when his father woke him three hours later.

Two deputations formed up the next morning. The first was made up of Mrs Reeves, Bob Marl, Harry Dobbs and some of the other villagers, who made their way to the Vicarage. The second was made up of Jack, Clare and Thomas, who made their way to Viviper Cottage.

Bob Marl had been elected spokesman for the first deputation. Mr Weever showed no signs of tiredness after his midnight expeditions.

'You see, vicar,' said Bob, 'we can't have that sort of going-on. Not all that noise we had last night. We've got to get these people stopped.'

The vicar waited for more.

The man who had tried to open the lorry doors spoke next. He was quite young, eager to please.

'We know you'd like to help, vicar,' he said. 'And it would help to get settled here. Make people see you were interested in the village. We need someone to head up a protest.'

'Like yesterday?' asked Mr Weever with a smile.

The man looked away, embarrassed. 'No,' he said. 'That was a bit stupid. We should have thought first.'

'It certainly hasn't helped your case,' said Mr Weever.

Mrs Reeves was unable to stop herself from talking any longer. 'If you'd only helped,' she said, 'things might have worked out better.'

'Put myself in front of the lorry?' he asked. 'I know I'm big, but even I can't stop a lorry.'

'No, but . . .' she said.

'And I don't see how it would have helped for me to get involved in your brawl. Who would trust me after that?'

'I'm not stopping here to be talked to like this,' she threatened. But she did.

'It seems to me,' he said, 'that there's precious little anyone can do. They own the Manor. They have permission to use it. They haven't started any work yet, they're just setting up, filling the cages, decorating, equipping. But when they do it won't be anything to do with us.'

'But last night,' said Bob. 'We can't have that noise.'

'I don't suppose that will happen again,' said the vicar. 'When they're settled. I imagine something just disturbed the dogs.'

Harry Dobbs shook his stick. 'You're vicar,' he said. 'You should stop them. Vicar always took the lead here. You should.'

'I've tried to explain, Harry,' said Mr Weever.

'Don't you soft-soap me,' said Harry. 'Vicar has the right to go in the Manor whenever he wants. That's so, isn't it?'

Mr Weever hesitated. 'Yes,' he agreed. 'In a sense.'

'What?' demanded Mrs Reeves. 'What do you mean, Harry?'

'You ask him,' said Harry. 'He knows. I'm going, if he won't help.'

And he stamped out.

The others waited.

'All it is,' said Mr Weever, 'is that whoever is

vicar of the village has right of access to the manor house at all times. For ever. He has no other power. It's tied up in the freehold. It seems that it always was like that, by tradition. But Miss Jane Gwyer had it put in writing in 1780, just before she disappeared.'

'Well,' said Mrs Reeves. Her podgy face grew rounder and squashier than ever. 'So that's your game. You know all about it. You sold it to them.'

'It was sold a year ago,' said Mr Weever. 'Before I arrived. They've been making plans, getting permission, that sort of thing.'

'But you knew?'

'Yes, I knew. When I accepted the parish. I knew then.'

'And you're hand in glove with them. Thank you very much.'

She stood up and waddled out. The others watched her. Bob Marl turned to the vicar.

'So that's it?' he said.

'In law, yes. I'm afraid so.'

'I'll thank you for your time, vicar,' he said, with no suggestion of gratitude. 'At least we know where we stand now.'

'Do we?' asked Mr Weever.

'I think so. I'll bid you goodbye.'

'Ah, the angel. And the heavenly host with him. I thought you might bring your cronies,' said Miss Aylmer when the second deputation arrived

72

at Viviper Cottage. 'Well, you'd better all come in.'

When they stepped inside, Thomas drew in his breath sharply and was glad that he had not come alone.

It was the same room they had stood in the night before, but it was transformed.

'You haven't met my friends,' said Miss Aylmer.

Shakti was the only snake loose in the room, but in every corner there were glass tanks with snakes in them. They lay coiled in bundles, stretched on sticks, asleep, watchful, black, brown, green, striped, banded and patterned.

Jack stood away from Miss Aylmer as Shakti wound himself away from her and held out his beautiful head, swaying it from side to side.

'He's all right,' she promised. 'I milked him yesterday.'

Jack pretended to laugh. He could not take his eyes from the cobra.

'You what?' asked Clare.

'I drained the venom, the poison from his fangs yesterday. I do it every two weeks, so he's always safe. He couldn't hurt you.'

Clare kept close to Jack. 'Do you like them?' she asked Thomas.

Thomas was peering through the glass at a beautiful snake with a hooped pattern.

'What's this?' he asked.

73

'A banded krait.'

'It's lovely.'

'Ugh!' said Jack.

'Is it safe?' asked Clare.

'Not exactly,' Miss Aylmer's American voice seemed to mock with its careful solemnity. 'It's one of the most poisonous snakes in the world.'

'But you milk it,' said Jack. 'So it's all right.' He was surprised to find that his voice was louder than he had meant it to be.

'No,' she said. 'I only milk Shakti. He's my friend and I like to have him near me. The others are allowed to keep their poison.'

She had moved near to Thomas to explain about the krait.

'Thomas!' shouted Jack. 'Watch out.'

The hooded cobra had lifted itself away from Miss Aylmer and was slithering towards Thomas. He looked down and saw it slide on to his arm.

'Get it off,' warned Jack.

The snake was heavy on Thomas's arm. It made its way up and on to his shoulder. He felt its scaly skin on his neck, warm and dry. The forked tongue flickered by his ear.

'Shaki,' said Thomas, carefully.

'Shakti,' Miss Aylmer corrected him.

'Shakti,' he repeated.

The snake made a small hissing sound.

'It's going to bite you,' said Jack. 'Listen.'

74

'He's smelling Thomas,' said Miss Aylmer. 'Like a dog. Getting used to him. Have you found your dog yet?' she asked Clare.

'No,' said Clare startled.

'How did you know?' asked Jack. 'How did you know we lost Towser?'

'He's not with you,' she said. 'Nor yesterday. It's a small village. Things get noticed.'

'Where is he?' demanded Jack, rudely.

'I think you've got an idea about that,' she said.

Jack closed up.

'Are these all foreign?' asked Thomas. He was fondling Shakti comfortably now.

'Most of them,' she said. 'The tropical ones are the most beautiful, but I have a few American ones to remind me of home. And a small nest of wyverns, here.' She showed them a different tank. 'They come from round here.'

'Wyverns?' said Clare.

'Sorry, vipers,' Miss Aylmer corrected herself. 'I forget. I use the old word sometimes. Would you like some orange juice?'

Clare and Thomas accepted. Jack was certain it would have snake venom in it, milked from Shakti, and he refused.

'There were many vipers around here once,' she told them. 'But different ways of farming have destroyed places where they used to live. I breed them in here and let them out in the summer. I like to think of them where they should be.'

'Isn't that dangerous?' asked Jack.

'There's an old rhyme,' said Miss Aylmer. She paused, and then chanted in a stranger voice than usual:

'On yonder hill there sits a viper.
If I go near he, he'll bite I,
But he won't bite I,
'cause I won't go near he.'

Jack looked puzzled and Miss Aylmer laughed. 'They're safe enough if you leave them alone,' she said. 'They're timid creatures and they'll run from you. It's only if you creep up on a sleeping wyvern and frighten it that it'll bite you. And perhaps, if you're like Thomas here, they won't bite you even then. You never know.'

'What do you mean, like Thomas?' asked Clare.

Miss Aylmer nodded approvingly at the question. 'He's a Ketch, isn't he?'

'What difference does that make?' asked Clare.

'What does your father do?' Miss Aylmer asked Thomas.

'Dairyman for Bob Marl,' said Thomas.

'Good with cows, is he?'

'The best there is,' said Thomas, proudly.

'Of course. He's a Ketch. Ketchs can do anything with animals. Even wyverns. No snake ever bit a Ketch.'

Thomas stroked Shakti.

Jack kicked his toe against the leg of a chair. 'It's a tame snake,' he muttered.

'Would you like to hold him for a minute?' Miss Aylmer offered.

Jack shook his head.

'How do you know about Ketchs?' asked Thomas.

'It's all in the church,' said Miss Aylmer. 'Didn't you know?'

'No.'

'Look on the south wall, inside. The Kych Stone. Don't you know it?'

'Sort of,' said Thomas. 'I've never really looked.'

'You should,' said Miss Aylmer. 'Kych is Ketch. They weren't too bothered about spelling in those days. As long as the word looked about right.'

'Is that all?' asked Thomas. 'About Ketchs?'

'There are some old books,' said Miss Aylmer. 'Records and things. The vicar might know.'

Thomas pulled a face.

'You keep saying wyvern,' said Jack.

'So I do,' she agreed.

'Wyverns are dragons,' he said. 'Not vipers.'

'They're both,' said Clare. 'She said. Sorry. I mean, Miss Aylmer said. It's an old name

77

for vipers.'

'You're both right,' said Miss Aylmer before Jack could become a horrid older brother. 'It is the old name for viper, but it's also the name for those dragons on the Manor gate. Two legs, not four like the Chinese dragon. A barbed tail and feet like an eagle.'

'The village is full of them,' said Clare. 'On the Manor, on the banner in church, even the pub sign's a wyvern, not a proper dragon with four legs.'

Miss Aylmer did not answer.

'That's just a coincidence,' said Jack. 'It's because the Gwyers used the wyvern for their badge, and they were the lords of the manor. So you get wyverns everywhere in the village. That's all.'

'It's a good idea,' said Miss Aylmer.

'But why did they have it as their badge in the first place?' asked Thomas.

Miss Aylmer looked pleased.

'Got to be something,' said Jack.

'But why a wyvern?' asked Clare, enjoying baiting a big brother.

'And the church,' said Miss Aylmer. 'There are carved wyverns in there.'

'Same reason,' said Jack. 'The church was owned by the Gwyers.'

'Sort of,' agreed Miss Aylmer. 'But the church was here first, three hundred years before the

Gwyers built the Manor. The wyverns were here then.'

'So that's why the Gwyers used wyverns,' said Jack, triumphantly. 'Because they were in the church.'

Clare and Thomas puzzled about this for a moment while Miss Aylmer waited.

At last Clare worked it out.

'But why were they in the church in the first place?' she asked. 'Answer that.'

Jack stopped smiling his smug smile.

'Because there were wyverns here before the church?' asked Miss Aylmer.

'Where?' said Thomas. 'It's the oldest building here.'

'Oh, not carved,' said Miss Aylmer. 'Real wyverns. Living here.'

Jack laughed openly. 'There aren't real wyverns,' he said.

'Would you like to hold Shakti,' offered Thomas, who was getting bored with the argument.

Jack leaped away and went white. 'Keep off,' he said.

Clare laughed.

'Don't tease him,' said Miss Aylmer.

'I've got to go,' said Jack.

The others agreed.

'I'll get the parcel,' said Miss Aylmer. 'It's just something small, but I'd be grateful if you could give it to your mother for me.'

She handed Thomas a small packet wrapped in paper with dragons on it. Shakti slid back to her. Thomas was sad to feel the warm weight leave him.

'Watch out for the wyverns,' Miss Aylmer warned them as they left.

TEN

'She's horrible,' said Jack.

They found the bench on the village green. It was a mound of snow, blown by the wind into a humped drift. Jack kicked the snow away and climbed up. He stood and stared at Viviper Cottage. Thomas and Clare joined him. Thomas faced in the opposite direction and stared at the gates of Wivern Manor.

'She's weird,' said Clare, which wasn't quite

agreeing but wasn't arguing either.

'The snake was beautiful,' said Thomas.

'Ugh,' said Jack and this time Clare did agree with him.

'We'll never get in there,' said Thomas. 'Look at the guards.'

'We'll get the key,' said Jack. He turned and watched two uniformed guards patrolling the grounds of the Manor.

'They'll stop us as soon as we open the side gate,' said Clare.

'We could report them to the police,' said Thomas. 'Say we know they've got Towser.'

'We don't,' said Clare.

'Anyway,' said Jack, 'they'd deny it and the police would believe them before they believed us.' He started to cry. 'They've got Towser,' he said. 'They're doing experiments on him.'

'No, they're not,' said Clare. 'He's run off somewhere and got lost in the snow.'

'He's in there,' said Jack fiercely. 'I know he is.'

'I heard him barking,' said Thomas. 'It sounded like Towser. And it came from this direction.'

'No,' said Clare. 'I don't believe it.'

Jack made a snowball and threw it at the sign. A guard approached and stared at them.

'I hate that place,' said Thomas. He jumped down from the bench. Miss Jane Gwyer stared over the white fields. 'And what about her?' he said. 'She used to live there. She must hate it, too. Listen.' He read aloud from the plinth, ' "All Creatures of the Hearth and Beasts of the Wild were her Friends and knew no Fear where she was, or where She Is Now." Now they're torturing animals in her house. She'd hate it.'

'She disappeared,' said Clare. 'Like Towser.'

'And no one ever saw her again,' said Thomas.

'Oh, shut up!' said Jack. 'We'll find him. We will! Tonight.'

'I can't tonight,' said Thomas. 'I've got to go and see Mum. In the hospital.'

'That's too early,' said Jack. 'In the middle of the night. Two o'clock.'

'It's Christmas Eve,' objected Clare.

'Good,' said Jack. 'There'll be no one about. The guards will be asleep.'

'Or drunk,' said Thomas. 'All grown-ups get drunk on Christmas Eve.'

'Better still,' said Jack.

'They've taken the bait,' said Mr Weever. 'There's a light on in the church.'

'I was right about that boy,' said Miss Aylmer. 'Shakti went straight to him. He's one of the family.'

'I knew it,' said Mr Weever. 'As soon as I heard him sing. They could always sing.'

'They needed to,' said Miss Aylmer.

'They still do,' he said.

'Yes. Is the dog safe? Towser.'

'I fed him an hour ago,' said Mr Weever. 'He's very annoyed. He doesn't like being shut up.'

'They won't find him, will they?'

'No chance of that.'

'Let's go, then.'

'All right,' he said. 'I think I'll tease them a bit. Tell them about Romanus.'

They laughed.

Mr Weever left Viviper Cottage and made his way through the dark to the church.

It had not been difficult finding the key.

The lights in the church were not by the door as they would be in a sensible house, and it was dusk when the three children went in. They had chosen to wait until it was nearly dark so that they would not be seen, but they had forgotten that the church was much darker than the outside, so what had been poor light in the snow-filled village was almost utter darkness in the church.

'Bother,' said Thomas. 'I know the switches are over on this wall.' He felt his way across, stumbled, saved himself and bumped into a pile of books, sending them sprawling.

'Should have brought a torch,' said Jack.

'We didn't think, did we? Ah. Here we are.'

Thomas lit the south aisle. Then the nave.

'Not that one,' said Clare. 'It's too much

They'll see us.'

'They'll see us anyway,' said Thomas, 'so we might as well be obvious. It's too late to worry about that now. Let's just be quick and get out.'

'Look,' said Clare. 'It's the Kych Stone.'

They gathered round and looked at the strangely carved stone set into the wall. Words were chiselled into it, but the letters were strange, and even the words that could be made out were not proper English.

'I can see "Kych",' said Clare.

'And "briddes",' said Jack. 'What's that? Brides?'

'Don't think so,' said Thomas. 'And "bestes". That must be beasts.'

'This is new,' said Clare. Below the stone and to the left, was a framed text. Thomas read aloud:

> *'Reach out and touch this carved stone*
> *If you are sick and would be whole.*
> *For Thomas Kych of Herpeton*
> *Has caused this tablet to be put*
> *Where all may use its potency.*
> *These birds and beasts that here are shewn*
> *And snakes, and creatures of the pond*
> *Will all conjoin at his command*
> *To heal all manner of disease*
> *That he has power to put away*
> *Through his familiarity*

With wyverns and with creatures all.
And if this remedy should fail,
Then seek out Master Kych, his book
And he will give you remedy.'

Thomas's voice echoed back at him when he finished.

'It doesn't say that,' said Jack, still looking at the stone.

'Here are the birds and the beasts,' said Clare. She traced her finger round the intricate carving at the edge of the stone. The patterns turned into proper shapes now that she knew what she was looking for.

'And creatures of the pond,' said Jack, touching a fish and a toad.

'And wyverns,' said Clare, whose hand had found a dragon.

'I can't make it out,' said Thomas. 'The words on the stone don't look like these words.'

'Some of them do,' said Clare.

Jack counted. 'Fifteen lines,' he said. 'That's the same.'

'C. Weever,' said Thomas, reading the name at the bottom corner of the framed text. 'He's written it.'

'Copied it,' said Clare.

'Translated it,' said Thomas importantly. 'But we can't hang about. Someone's going to see the light on in here soon. Get the key.'

Jack watched the door while Thomas found the small cupboard with the keys hanging in it. They were all labelled things like 'Flower Cupboard' and 'Altar Frontals', and there was a large old key that he was sure he had never seen in there before. It had a new label that read 'Wivern Manor'.

'Got it,' he hissed.

'Come on, then,' said Clare.

'Someone coming,' said Jack.

'Lights out,' said Clare.

'No! Leave them on,' said Thomas. 'Look normal.'

They looked perfectly villainous when Mr Weever came in. Thomas was studying a brass on the floor by the Lady Chapel. Clare was reading a hymn book. Jack was standing with his hands behind his back looking up at the roof. Any teacher would have known at once that they were up to something. They kept well away from the Kych Stone.

'Hello,' said the vicar. 'I thought I must have left the light on by mistake. Fancy you being in here.'

'We were just going,' said Clare.

'You look pretty settled to me,' he said. He stood in the doorway so that they could not get out.

'No, we've got to go,' said Jack.

'Early night tonight?' he asked innocently.

Jack yawned. 'Yes. Really.'

'You'll be in church tomorrow morning, then? Christmas.'

'Oh, yes.'

'I thought next year we might have a service at midnight. They do in lots of places.'

'Yes. Really good idea,' said Jack. 'We'll come to that. Well, good night.'

Mr Weever did not move away from the door.

'And in October we could have the St Romanus procession.'

'That's good, too,' said Jack.

'Oh, I'm glad you agree,' said the vicar. 'I thought it would be new to the village, but you must have done it before.'

'No, I don't think so,' said Thomas. He was holding the key behind his back.

'Tell him what happens, Jack,' said Mr Weever.

'What?'

'In the procession.'

'Oh, sorry, I didn't understand. I don't know.'

He's making fun of us, thought Clare. 'Please tell us,' she said.

'Well, it's great fun. I'm sure they must have done it here hundreds of years ago, but it's died out. They do it in Rouen, where St Romanus came from, so I think they must have done it here in St Romanus' Church. On 23 October, St Romanus' Day, you have a great procession, people carry models of dragons round the village, and the models are set alight so that it looks as though they're breathing fire. It's very impressive.'

'Dragons?' said Thomas.

'Yes. Though I suppose we should use wyverns here, don't you?' He stepped aside to let them pass. 'I mustn't keep you,' he said. 'I'm sure you've lots to do.'

They heard his huge laugh as they ran down the path.

'I hate him,' said Jack.

Clare agreed and looked at Thomas, who said, 'I'm not sure any more. I'll see you later. I'm going to the hospital.'

'Two o'clock,' said Jack. 'At the gate.'

ELEVEN

'I'm sorry about all this,' said Thomas's father on the way home from the hospital.

Thomas wanted to say 'It's not your fault', to make his father feel better, but he couldn't speak.

'I'll make it up to you,' he promised. 'We both will. When your mum's better.'

Mrs Ketch had looked very ill when Thomas arrived. She had been for some special treatment and she was tired. She talked for a little while but then she fell asleep while Thomas was still there. She had never done that before.

Thomas left the little parcel with the dragon paper next to her bed. He kissed her lightly and left with his father.

'It won't be much of a Christmas,' said Mr Ketch. Thomas concentrated on the road in the car's headlights. 'We've got all your presents, though,' he said. 'So don't worry about that.'

'Can I take them to the hospital and open them there?'

"Course you can. Mum'll like that.' But he wasn't sure as he looked at the night.

New snow fell, closing up the road behind them.

'Village'll be sealed off, I reckon,' said Mr Ketch. 'We'll be lucky to get through.'

A guard looked through the gates of the Manor at them as the car made its slow progress through the deep snow by the village green. A big dog leaped up and planted its paws on the curled iron.

There was no sound from inside the big house.

'I'll have an early night,' said Thomas. 'Good night.'

'See you in the morning.'

Thomas set his alarm for one thirty and lay thinking about his mother's thin smile as he had arrived and the loose pains on her sleeping face as he had left the ward. He did not know any more until the buzzer woke him hours later.

The wyverns spread hungry grins into the night. Thomas looked up at them as he passed. Then he waited at the side gate of the Manor, hoping that Jack and Clare would not come. The sky had spilled down all its snow and now the stars leaped in its clear blackness. He stood right against the flint wall so that he would be invisible if anyone passed. What a stupid idea! Who walks in graveyards after midnight, except for ghosts? Thomas shuddered, then he grinned. And Father Christmas, he decided. He was not able to stop himself looking up into the sky to see if he could see a sleigh and reindeer. Funny how you keep on looking for things after you've stopped believing in them.

'Looking for Santa?' whispered Jack, and he laughed silently.

Thomas was glad that it was too dark for them to see him blush.

'Let's go,' said Jack.

He put the cold key into the keyhole. It turned silently, smoothly.

'Funny,' he said. 'I thought it'd creak. They must keep it oiled.'

'I've never seen anyone use it till the other day,' said Clare.

'Shh. Let's go in.'

They were not prepared for the bright security

lights that swamped them with a yellow wash.

'Keep to the side,' warned Jack.

Thomas and Clare did not need to be told. They sprinted across the yard and hugged the side of the house.

'Round the back,' said Jack. They followed the line of the wall and turned a corner. It was darker there where the Manor looked out over the fields, towards the Barrow.

Jack clutched Clare's arm and motioned to her. She followed his sign and saw a small window open on the ground floor.

Thomas nodded, groaning silently. They were going in after all. It was all too easy to be true. He didn't trust it.

He need not have worried. As they drew near to the window, a cloud of blue smoke plumed out. The three children bumped into each other as they came to a sudden stop. A man's head appeared after the smoke. He raised a point of red light to his face. It glowed briefly, then he blew out more smoke. If he turned just a little to the right he would see them.

'Stopped snowing,' he said.

Thomas flinched.

'Sure?' asked a voice behind him.

'Come and see.'

But the other man did not bother.

Another red glow. Another blue cloud. The man threw his cigarette into the yard. The red light arced up and fell on the snow with a soft hiss. Thomas let his eyes follow it up, but he did not watch it fall. As he looked up he saw two great black birds fly over. They banked round to the left and went out of sight. Owls? Not crows, not at night, but they were rook-black. Then he remembered that all cats are black in the dark. The window slammed shut and he stopped thinking about it.

They waited a few minutes before they carried on, just in case. Everything was locked. A big door, bigger than the front door, looked over a sweep of stairs going down to the gardens at the back, but it was locked. As they went round, all windows and doors were secure. Thomas felt a mixture of disappointment and relief. It was a shame not to be able to get in, but he was frightened of what they might find, or who might find them if they did. They carried on round the house.

'They've taken down the wyverns,' whispered Clare when they reached the front.

The boys reached up. The gateposts were empty.

'But I saw them,' said Thomas. 'When I came across.'

'Must have got confused in the dark,' said Jack.

'Who's there?'

It was a voice from the window.

A door slammed.

Clare grabbed Thomas and pulled him after her. Jack overtook them. Their feet were silent in the snow.

They ran straight past their escape gate where the lights were bright, round the back of the house to the darkness, and crouched inside the heavy frame of the huge door at the top of the steps.

'They'll get us,' said Clare.

'We could split up,' suggested Thomas. 'I'll wait till they come round the corner. Then I'll run to the front. When they chase after me you two double back, unlock the gate and leave it open for me. I'll get there before they do. Lock it after me.'

'They'll catch you,' said Clare. 'It won't work.'

The voices were getting louder, nearer.

'Just a rat,' said the second voice.

'With these footprints?' asked the first.

'Get ready,' said Thomas. 'I'll step out into the open when they turn the corner.'

Click.

'We're in,' said Jack. He took his gate key from the lock, pushed the door and they fell in. He quickly locked it after him. They huddled, dead still in the darkness. A hand outside tried the handle. The door shook. The hand was removed. They waited, breathing deeply.

Thomas was shaking. 'What now?' he asked.

A thin beam of light pierced the gloom. Jack had switched on his pocket torch. 'We go and find Towser,' he said. The room they were in was full of computer screens and keyboards. But none of it was live. It had been delivered but not installed. The desks were tidy. There were no photographs, no diaries, no pot plants. The waste-paper bins still had labels stuck to the side and no rubbish in them.

'We can get out and make a run for the gate,' said Clare. 'They won't still be waiting out there.'

'Right,' agreed Thomas.

'I'll go through this way,' said Jack, ignoring them. 'Downstairs first, but upstairs too if I have to.' He stared at them. 'I can't give you the key to the gate because then I'll be stuck. You'll just have to wait here. You'll be safe enough.'

Thomas was angry at the contempt in Jack's voice.

'He's not here,' he said. 'That's why we should go. You know he's not here.'

'I'm going to find out,' said Jack.

'Then I'll come with you,' said Clare.

Thomas was not going to wait in that room on his own so he went too.

As soon as they stepped through the door they could smell the animals.

A great entrance hall, brighter than the back room because of the light thrown in from the bright sky, stood beneath the graceful sweep of an open staircase which seemed to hang unsupported in the air. There were four large doors off the hall, as well as the one through which the children had come, and a smaller one, which was locked.

'We'll try one each,' said Jack. Thomas and Clare decided otherwise, so they stuck together. Each door told the same story. Rows and rows of cages stretched away in lines. Eager faces bumped against the wire mesh. Clare put out a hand and touched a wet nose.

'Oh!' she said. 'It's terrible.'

'They look happy enough to me,' said Thomas.

Jack and Clare glared at him with black eyes. None of the dogs was Towser.

'All right,' agreed Thomas. 'They haven't got much room, but they're looked after, aren't they? And if it does people good, makes them well.'

'They haven't started yet,' said Jack. 'Can't you see? It's like those computers in the back. Nothing's plugged in yet.'

'We could let them out,' said Clare.

'Later,' said Jack. 'When we've been upstairs.'

They all felt very exposed climbing the wide staircase.

'This is no good,' said Thomas. 'Let's go.'

Jack led on. The corridors upstairs led off in two directions. The rooms here were smaller and there were many more of them, mostly empty.

'I thought I saw someone,' said Clare.

97

'Where?'

'Going round the corner. A woman.'

'Just a shadow,' said Jack. He stepped into another empty room. He was getting restless. 'There's no one in the house at all,' he said. 'And the guards don't know we're here. They're outside, or in their little room at the back. They don't know we've got a key.'

'We didn't look in their room,' said Thomas.

'Must be through the locked door,' said Clare. 'Servants' quarters.'

'What if Towser's with them?'

'He won't be,' said Jack. 'Come on.'

More stairs, narrow ones, led higher still. Jack's torch lit the way through the dark places where the starlight did not shine in. Their feet were noisy on the uncarpeted boards. They slowed down, tiptoed, stopped.

'Shh,' said Clare.

Footsteps, slow and steady, continued ahead of them.

'Let's go,' said Thomas.

'The attics,' said Jack. 'We've still got to look in the attics.'

The footsteps continued above them.

'Can't you hear?' said Clare. 'Let's go.'

They tumbled down the stairs, rattling their feet now, not bothering to be quiet. They reached the corridor and ran straight into the figure of an old man.

'Gotcha!'

Jack darted to his left. The others followed him. They were in an empty bedroom. The door slammed behind them. A bolt screeched. Jack ran back and rattled the handle.

'We're locked in,' he said.

'That's right,' croaked an old voice. 'Locked in. And you'll stay here while I get Nigel and Ted.'

'Look, we're only here for a bet,' said Jack. 'Let us out.'

'Oh, yes?'

'We don't even come from round here,' he said. 'It's just a bet.'

'Oh, and you didn't throw snowballs at the sign the other day. And you didn't come in the side gate. And you don't go round with the carol singers neither, I expect,' said the old man. 'I seen you. And I know what to do with you.'

'Get the police,' said Thomas. 'We're burglars. Send for the police.'

The man laughed again. 'Think I'm stupid?' he asked. 'I'll not send for the police. Don't want no one looking round here. Not at what goes on. You know.'

'No, we don't,' said Clare. 'We don't know anything.'

'All the beasties,' said the man. 'You know what we're going to do with the beasties. The police don't want to know about all that, do they?'

'What?' demanded Clare. 'What do you get up to with them?'

'Projects,' said the man. 'When the work starts. After Christmas. Special projects.'

'For medicine,' said Thomas. 'That's all right.'

'Gaah,' said the old man.

'Make-up,' said Clare. 'Testing cosmetics.'

'Waste of time,' said the old man. 'We got no time for that.'

'What then?' asked Jack.

'You knows. That's why you're here. You knows, all right. Young Master Ketch. He knows.'

Clare and Jack looked at Thomas.

'I don't know,' he mouthed silently.

'Where's Towser?' said Jack suddenly.

'What?'

'My dog. What have you done with him?'

The old man cackled. 'Had an accident, maybe,' he said. 'Lots of accidents happen. Don't 'em? Eh? Like your accident.'

'Which accident?' said Clare. But she had a terrible feeling that she knew already, so she was not surprised when she heard the answer.

'Hasn't happened yet,' said the creaky voice. 'But it will. When Nigel and Ted come. It'll happen then.'

And his feet faded along the corridor.

TWELVE

'What was all that about?' Jack demanded.

'Search me,' said Thomas.

'Young Master Ketch?'

'Yes?'

'What do you know?'

Jack was staring fiercely at Thomas and his hands were clenched into fists.

'He doesn't know anything,' said Clare. 'Leave him alone.'

Jack pushed her away. 'That old man knows him,' he said. 'How?'

'I don't know,' said Thomas.

'You didn't want to come here tonight, did you?'

'No,' admitted Thomas.

'Neither did I,' said Clare. 'It was a stupid idea. I knew Towser wasn't here.'

'You shut up,' said Jack with that special kind of rudeness he reserved for his younger sister. 'And you didn't want to let the animals out,' he said to Thomas. 'You wanted them left in there for the experiments.'

'For medicine,' said Thomas. 'That was when I thought it was for medicine.'

'What difference does it make?'

'You stupid,' said Clare. 'His mum. She's ill. They've got to make her better.'

Jack began to tell her to shut up again, but he thought better of it. There was something in the look on her face and something in what she had said that made him stop. 'It's still wrong,' he said. 'Even if it is for medicine.'

'The point is,' said Thomas, 'it isn't, and I don't know any more about what's going on here than you do. And I want those animals free as well, now.'

'And I want us free,' said Clare.

This reminder that they were in perhaps more danger than the animals brought the argument

102

to an end.

'Try the window,' suggested Jack.

But they were too high to jump to safety. There was no ledge, no down pipe, no ivy to climb down. Two dark birds circled in a dark sky. Thomas frowned.

'This looks a good place for an accident,' said Clare, looking down.

'Look,' said Jack.

'It's that woman,' said Clare. 'The one I saw up here.'

A woman in an old-fashioned buttoned jacket and a long skirt walked past the house underneath them. She stopped, looked up at the sky and watched the two birds. Then she looked up at the window where the children stood, but she gave no sign of seeing them. Her black figure stood out against the snow, but they were lost in shadow.

'It's Jane Gwyer,' said Jack.

'What?' asked Clare.

'The statue. It's her.'

'Don't be stupid,' said Clare.

'No,' said Thomas. 'It's not Miss Gwyer. She's still there.' He indicated the bronze figure where it stood on the village green with its back turned to them. They looked back down at the snow beneath them and the woman was gone.

Footsteps rattled on the stairs. The children could hear deep voices, a creaking laugh.

'We've got to hide,' said Clare. 'They're coming.'

'They can't do anything to us,' said Jack. 'They wouldn't dare.'

'Master Ketch!' called the old voice.

'Yes.'

'We want you to come with us.'

'Where?' asked Thomas.

'Just for a little ride with your friends.'

'What are you doing here?' asked Jack.

'Ask Master Ketch.'

'He won't tell us.'

'No,' said the old voice. 'Ketchs don't tell a lot.'

'You tell, then,' said Jack.

'We want to find a wyvern,' said the old man. 'What else would anyone do in Herpeton?' And he laughed.

Clare gaped. 'He's mad,' she whispered.

'What's that?' demanded the old voice, although he could not possibly have heard her. 'Mad, is it? Ask Master Ketch.'

Jack glared at Thomas again.

'You'll be in trouble,' said Clare. 'When your boss comes after Christmas and finds out what's been going on.'

'Boss?' The old man laughed. 'What am I, then?'

'A caretaker,' said Jack.

The old man laughed again. The children had never heard so much laughter with so little joy.

'Oh, I'm boss enough for this place,' said the old man. 'And I'm caretaker enough, too. I'll take care of you three before Master Ketch can start any trouble.'

'Come on,' said a deeper voice. 'Let's get it done.'

'You'll wait till I tell you,' snapped the old man. 'It's your dog you're after, is it?' he called through the door.

'You've got him, haven't you?' said Jack. 'Where is he?'

'Dead,' said the old man. 'At the bottom of an exploration shaft in the Barrow. One of the tunnels they dug to find the king. He fell down it and died.'

'No,' said Clare.

Thomas was looking round the room, hoping to find a way out, a place to hide. He grabbed the handle of a large cupboard door and turned it. The door would not budge.

'Oh, yes,' mocked the voice. 'And that's where you'll find him.'

'You threw him down there,' said Jack.

Thomas tugged at the handle.

'Perhaps I did,' said the old man. 'You never know. When you get there, you can ask him.' This seemed to him to be the funniest thing so far and he laughed until he was overcome with a coughing fit.

Thomas strained at the door, his feet sliding

towards it with effort. Suddenly it came free and he staggered back.

'Nigel and Ted will take you there,' the old man said when he was calm enough to speak again. 'Won't you, boys? And they'll help you down.'

The children heard a bolt being drawn on the other side of the door, but they paid little attention. Their eyes were fixed on the cupboard that Thomas had opened. He backed away quickly as something hissed at him. Clare gave a small sobbing noise and Jack screamed openly.

'No good screaming,' warned the voice. 'No one here to hear you. Drat this bolt. You try it, Ted. It's stuck.'

A long shiny snake slid out of the cupboard, rose up and fanned out the skin round its head into a smooth hood. It hissed.

But it was the other snakes that had frightened Clare and Jack. Dozens, scores, perhaps over a hundred small serpents twisted out and into the room. They hissed quietly and pushed out their thin, forked tongues. They shone with a dull glow in the starlight and their bodies were beautiful with a lozenge pattern.

'Shakti?' asked Thomas.

The hooded snake slid over to him as if in answer. He picked it up and let it run round his neck.

Jack moved towards the window, frightened to

106

make any sudden action lest he attract the vipers. He looked as though he would throw himself to the ground outside if they came near him. But they gathered together by the door, writhing.

'I can give you wyverns,' said Thomas suddenly as he remembered the old name for vipers.

The noise of the struggle with the bolt stopped.

'I know that,' said the man. 'I want no wyverns from you. That's why you've got to go.'

With a slam the bolt slid free.

The door swept open, scattering the snakes at the front.

The old man leered in at the three children. He did not let his eyes look down at the floor.

'Come on, then,' he ordered them. 'Out you get.'

Thomas held his arm forward, Shakti rearing up.

The room was in darkness and the passageway lit, so the children could see out clearly but they were nearly invisible to the three men.

'Come and get us,' said Thomas.

As if in support of this demand the snakes began to hiss all together.

The old man stepped back.

'What's that?' he said. His voice was less certain than it had been.

'Come and see,' said Thomas.

From the window, Jack looked at his friend in

107

amazement.

The snakes began to squirm through the door.

The old man shrieked. 'Get them!' he shouted. 'Get them!'

His two assistants jumped back.

The old man lifted his feet and stamped heavily, trying to snap the snakes beneath his boots, but they darted away from him and then sprang back. His attempts to drive them off looked like a comic dance, but the expression of hatred on his face took away any temptation to laugh.

Nigel and Ted turned and ran, ignoring his commands to get the children.

Thomas stepped forward from the room and looked at the old man. He held out his arm and threatened him with Shakti. The cobra reared up, spread his hood and hissed.

'Let us go,' said Thomas, 'or I'll let him bite you.'

Jack and Clare got ready to make a run for it when the old man stepped back, but he didn't move. His face split into a wicked grin. He lifted his arm and pushed back his sleeve. Then, raising his bare arm, with his hand clenched into a fist, he brandished it at them.

Thomas and the others could see the purple tattoo of a snake, writhing on his skin. It was identical to the one on Weever's arm.

'Get back in there,' he said, savagely.

He kicked at the vipers, who squirmed away

from him. He reached forward to grab Shakti, but Thomas drew away quickly. Then the old man shoved him hard in the chest and sent him spinning back into the room.

'Your friends can't hurt me, Master Ketch,' he said, shaking his patterned forearm. 'You can wait here until those fools come back. Then we'll get you off to the Barrow before it begins to get light.'

Most of the vipers had disappeared down the corridors, but there were a few left in the room and Jack was still determined not to move from his place. He watched the old man kick the vipers away from him, and he hated him.

But not as much as Thomas hated him, because Thomas loved the snakes and was frightened they would be hurt.

The old man laughed to see how Thomas was upset.

'Or you could give me your book,' he said. 'And I'll let you free. You'd be in no danger then, would you? Eh? What about it? Give me your book and I'll let you all go.'

'No,' said Thomas. 'I won't.'

'Then you can go down the Barrow with your dead dog,' he snarled. He grabbed the door to swing it shut.

That was when Jack shouted and pointed.

THIRTEEN

The woman's long skirt brushed against the surface of the snow, but not enough to erase her small footprints. She paused when she heard the window open above her, but, looking up, she could not see anyone inside against the darkness. She moved on, pleasantly aware that in looking up her eyes had caught the outline of two dark shapes circling above her in the night sky.

She walked confidently through the locked

110

courtyard and round the side of the house until she met with another figure, also in a long black skirt. He nodded to her, held up his key and she smiled. The fields stretched away, snow-covered, silent.

'They're in there,' said Weever.

'Yes,' said Felicity Aylmer. 'I heard them open a window.'

'Is everything arranged?'

'I sent Shakti in earlier, with the others. He knows his way round the gaps in those panelled walls. He'll find him.'

'They're on the wing,' said Weever.

'Yes. I saw them just now.'

'After all this time,' he said, in a wondering voice.

'Just as well,' said Miss Aylmer.

'Does he know he's done it?'

'I don't think so. Not yet. But he'll know soon. And then he'll be really dangerous.'

'Yes,' agreed Weever. 'Are we going in?'

Miss Aylmer nodded. 'In a minute,' she said. 'Open the door.'

Weever opened the door.

'Both doors,' she said. 'Wide.'

Weever stooped to unfasten the bolt. The skirt of his cassock brushed the floor. The doorway gaped wide.

'Stand well away,' she said.

They moved back from the door, their feet

crunching the snow.

'A little further, I think,' said Miss Aylmer. 'I wouldn't want to be too close.'

'If they come,' said Weever.

Ted and Nigel carried on running until they had reached their little room. Nigel slammed the door and locked it. Ted threw himself into a chair, panting.

'They chased us,' said Nigel.

Ted would have agreed if he could have spoken.

'Horrible things,' said Nigel.

Ted did not argue.

'We shouldn't be here,' said Nigel. 'Not if there's snakes.'

Ted blew his nose with a shaking hand. 'We can't leave,' he managed to say at last.

'I'm not staying.'

'He'll follow us,' said Ted. 'You know he will. He'll get us put into prison again.'

Nigel looked wounded. 'He'll go as well,' he said. 'We'll tell.'

'Nothing to tell,' said Ted. 'He's done nothing wrong. He's been careful about that. We've done it all.'

'He made us. He paid us,' said Nigel.

'Only our word,' said Ted. 'And they won't believe us. Not seeing as we've already been in prison before, and he hasn't.' He lit a cigarette and dragged on it deeply. It made him cough a lot, but he looked happier when he had recovered.

'I don't want to do nothing to hurt kids,' said Nigel. 'We never said we'd do that.'

'It's them or us,' said Ted.

'I'd rather go to prison,' said Nigel.

Ted thought about this. 'Maybe,' he half agreed. 'Maybe. But it won't just be prison, will it? Think on. Think what he can do to us.'

Nigel thought. 'He does horrible things,' he said.

'Think what he might do,' Ted urged him.

'All right,' said Nigel. 'I'll take the kids down to that shaft. But I won't push them down it. He'll have to do that himself.'

'He'll do it,' Ted promised him. 'He'll do that all right.'

'And I won't have nothing to do with no snakes,' said Nigel. 'He'll have to get rid of them first.'

'He will,' said Ted. 'He'll get rid of them.' The cigarette had made him more cheerful and confident. 'I expect they'll have gone already,' he said. 'We'd best go back and see.' He stood up and pulled the front of his jacket down to smarten himself up. 'Open that door.'

Nigel opened it, hesitantly. He looked down at the floor for snakes. 'All clear,' he said. 'So far.'

He opened the door fully and looked up.

Then he screamed.

They were larger than Weever had expected, and he was glad that Miss Aylmer had made him stand back.

One moment they were high in the sky, the next, with terrifying swiftness they were swooping down towards the open doors. Weever flinched.

'They're huge,' he whispered. One of them turned its face to him and let its mouth gape. A forked tongue flickered for a moment, then disappeared. The second settled beside it. Their claws scraped against the paving stones. All around them snow melted in an instant. Weever stepped back further, but Miss Aylmer stood her ground.

They folded their wings and half stepped, half slid into the house.

'Smoke,' shouted Jack. 'Fire!'

The old man turned and followed the line of Jack's pointing finger with his eyes. Blue smoke was curling in the air at the top of the staircase. A look of panic flashed over his face. He slammed the door shut and rammed the bolt home.

'Fire!' shouted Jack. He ran across the floor, clear of snakes now, and hammered his fist against the door. 'Fire! You can't lock us in here now. Fire!'

'Better still,' the old man shouted through the door. 'Better still. No evidence at all. All burned.'

His footsteps disappeared up the passageway.

His face twisted with fear. He stopped, sniffed, paused, sniffed again at the blue smoke. 'Perfume,' he muttered. 'Smells like perfume.' Then he moved cautiously forward again.

The dogs' howling carried over the snow. Lights clicked on in houses all around the green.

'Wave out of the window,' said Clare. 'They'll see us. Someone will see us.'

'No, they won't,' said Jack. 'Not up here, in the dark. They'll never see us.'

Thomas stroked Shakti. The hooded cobra smoothed its body along his arm and round his neck.

'Get that thing away from me,' said Jack.

'Sorry,' apologised Thomas, who had genuinely forgotten that Jack was frightened of Shakti.

'We'll burn,' said Clare, 'if we don't do something.'

'We could kick the door down,' said Jack.

On television it always looked easy to kick a door down. This door was thick and heavy and fastened well. Jack grabbed his foot after the first kick and he didn't try again.

Blue smoke curled under the door.

'This is it,' said Jack. 'And it's all your fault,' he said to Thomas. 'You got us into this.'

'But you said Towser was in here,' Thomas protested.

'They didn't want Towser at all,' said Jack. 'They wanted you all the time. You and your book.'

'I don't think so,' said Thomas. 'They weren't expecting us. And they don't know whether I've got a book or not, do they?'

'What do you mean?' asked Clare.

'Well,' explained Thomas, 'they want to throw us down the Barrow or let us burn in here so I can't get the book. If I'd got it, they'd save us, so that I could give it to them.'

Jack leaped up. He hammered at the door again.

'Let us out!' he shouted. 'He'll give you the book. We've got it here. Let us out, or the book will burn with us.'

He choked as he shouted. The smoke was catching at the back of his throat. He turned and glowered at them. 'Come on,' he said. 'You shout, too. It's our only hope.'

Thomas kicked the door, less hard than Jack had. Clare shouted. 'We'll give you the book,' they called. 'Let us out! The book's here!'

To their surprise they heard the bolt being drawn back again. The door opened.

Nigel took one look at the beasts in the corridor with the blue smoke curling out of their cruel mouths, then he turned, pushed Ted out of the way and climbed out through the tiny window. It was a tight fit, and with Ted pushing him from behind he tore his uniform jacket. Ted was thinner than Nigel and he was through more quickly. They set off together blindly, jumping the low wall at the back of the house and plunging through the fresh snow in the fields beyond.

The beasts trailed sharp tails through the house. Their feet were clumsy on the stairs, but they helped themselves up with the aid of their wings. The blue smoke grew thicker and thicker.

Miss Aylmer plucked Weever by the sleeve and took him with her into the house after them.

'Will they find him?' asked Weever.

'I should think so,' said Miss Aylmer. 'Look at this.'

She opened a door and saw the rows of cages.

'Poor things,' she said.

Weever scouted round and found a metal rod. He jammed it into the lock and forced it open. The dogs jumped down and capered round. They howled with delight to be free and the others joined in, begging to be let loose too.

Weever went along the row, forcing all the locks. Then he did the other rooms. There seemed to be hundreds of the dogs. They jumped and howled and yapped and bayed with joy. Some ran upstairs, some stayed in the wide hall. Most sniffed the air and followed the cool scent into

117

the open.

'They won't go far,' said Miss Aylmer. 'We'll be able to round them up tomorrow.'

Weever was panting with the effort of forcing the locks, but he looked happy and eager for something else to do.

'Upstairs?' he said.

'Do you think we should?'

'I don't know. But I want to see.'

'All right.'

The carpet was singed and there were deep gouges in the wood of the stair rail. Weever and Miss Aylmer turned the corner at the top of the stairs and looked around. They were surprised to see that it was empty, save for a few dogs. The smoke was very thick up there.

'Can you hear that?' asked Weever.

'This way,' said Miss Aylmer.

The banging grew louder and then they could hear voices as well.

'We'll give you the book,' someone promised.

Weever drew back the bolt and pushed the door open.

'Good,' he said. 'I want that book. Where is it?'

Jack and Clare stared at him. Thomas narrowed his eyes and licked his lips, like a snake.

FOURTEEN

The old man moved forward towards the blue
smoke. He reached the bend in the passageway
just as the first wyvern reached the top of the
stairs. They gazed at each other with loathing.

The wyvern opened its mouth and breathed
out. A plume of fire burned the floor in front of
it. The old man turned, ran clumsily back the
way he had come, wrenched open a door and
clattered down an iron fire escape. The wyverns

sprang after him, but the narrow passageway slowed them down and they could not keep up with him. All the advantages of their size and strength were turned against them. By the time they had scraped their way to the opening, the man was long gone. They stepped out into the night, launched themselves into the air and circled high into the night, their keen eyes searching the snow-covered fields.

Ted and Nigel were ready to fall down exhausted into the snow but the beagles started to catch up with them. They snapped at the men's heels and drove them on.

'Split up,' said Nigel, but when they separated, the dogs forced them back together. The men soon realised that they were no longer running blindly, but were being driven, they had no idea where. If they slowed down, the dogs nipped them and hurried them on. If they turned, the dogs skirted round them and turned them back. Their feet were heavy with tiredness and with snow. They gasped for breath. But the dogs gave them no rest. A circle of stones loomed ahead of them. Ted tried to run round it. The dogs turned him. Nigel broke through first, then Ted. The dogs hung back. The stones enclosed a space the size of a large house. Ted and Nigel found that they could walk wherever they wanted inside the circle and the dogs left them alone. As soon as they tried to step outside, the dogs snapped at them and drove them back. No dog would go inside the stone circle.

Ted sank down and rested his back against a stone. 'May as well stay here a bit,' he said.

'Not much choice,' said Nigel.

The old man kept his eyes high as he ran across the fields. He knew he had a good start on the wyverns but he also knew how fast they would be once they took to the air. There was no shelter for him, no hiding place out in the open against the snow, but he knew that there was no safety in the woods or undergrowth. The only way to his sanctuary was over open countryside. His legs ached and he had a pain in his side well before he was even halfway there. His throat was hot and bitter and he saw the wyverns high above him.

The noise of dogs baying confused him and he stumbled in the wrong direction for a few paces. Then he saw that Parcel's Stones were nearer than he had thought. He plunged forward. A wyvern swooped. He heard the harsh sound of its wings and felt the heat of its breath. He kicked a dog out of his way and thought that the wyvern had turned early to avoid hurting the beagle. The dogs snapped at him. A second wyvern swooped, but he was there now. He banged into a tall stone, hurting his shoulder. He cried out

121

in pain and tripped, kicking a startled Nigel.

The wyverns circled high over them, round the edge of the stone circle, never crossing it, even in the air.

'You fools,' the old man snarled when he saw the two guards. 'You'll be sorry you ran away.'

All around the circle dogs kept watch. The wyverns banked in the air, flapped slow wings and flew off.

'He hasn't got it,' said Miss Aylmer. 'Have you?' she asked Thomas.

'No.'

'I thought not,' said Weever.

Shakti slid down from Thomas's arm and slithered across to Miss Aylmer.

'You were upstairs,' said Clare looking at Miss Aylmer's long skirt and tight jacket. 'Earlier. I saw you.'

'And we heard your footsteps,' said Jack.

'We came in together,' said Weever. 'Just now.'

'We're going to burn to death,' said Jack, 'if we don't get out.'

'I don't think so,' said Weever. 'But we'll get out anyway.'

'The fires have flown,' said Miss Aylmer, looking at Thomas.

'What about the snakes?' he asked her.

'They'll be safe enough,' she said. 'They'll get home.'

'But how did they get here?' asked Clare.

Jack ran his finger over the charred wooden panelling of the staircase as they descended.

'I suppose Shakti led them in,' said Miss Aylmer.

'How did this happen?' asked Jack, showing his blackened finger to the vicar.

'Scorched,' he answered.

The carpet ash clung to their feet.

'Better go round the side gate,' said Weever. 'Got the key?' he asked Thomas.

Jack produced it from his pocket.

But the gate was unlocked.

The lights were mostly out in the houses when the five of them regained the village green. Old Harry Dobbs stood alone beneath the statue of Jane Gwyer.

'Morning, Harry,' said Weever.

'I knowed,' he said. 'Soon as you arrived, I knowed.'

'You didn't trust me, though,' said Weever.

'Doesn't do to trust no one,' said Harry.

'No,' agreed Weever.

'Not till you see what they'm up to.'

'Would you like a drink, Mr Dobbs?' asked Miss Aylmer.

He looked at her for a long time before he answered. 'Not yet,' he said, at last. 'I still doesn't know what you'm up to.'

'No,' said Miss Aylmer. 'Not yet.'

'Where is he?' asked Harry. He motioned towards the Manor.

'Who?' asked Weever.

'Parcel.'

'Parcel?' repeated Thomas, who had been paying very close attention to this strange conversation.

'I expect he's in his stones,' said Weever. 'It's the only place he'll be safe tonight.'

Harry laughed. 'They'll be back soon,' he said. They followed his eyes to the empty gateposts. 'I never thought to see 'em,' he said. 'Not after all this time.'

'Dangerous times,' said Weever. 'You need help in dangerous times.'

Harry spoke to Thomas. 'You be careful, young Master Ketch,' he warned. 'You just be careful how you do fetch out the wyverns.'

Before Thomas could answer, Harry turned and walked off. 'Good night to you all,' he called.

'What's all that about?' asked Jack.

'Tomorrow,' said Weever. 'Time enough for that tomorrow. It's late.'

Although it was late, Weever did not go back to his own house but went with Miss Aylmer into Viviper Cottage. Jack and Clare were in trouble when they got home.

'I don't know what it's all about,' said their mother. 'But you're too old to be babies about Christmas Eve and too young to go out. It's lucky for you your father's slept through it all.'

'We went looking for Towser,' said Jack, truthfully enough.

Thomas's father didn't ask him anything. He sat beside the blue bleak embers of the fire, waiting. Thomas sat next to him. A small heat, but no glow seeped out of the embers.

'Sorry,' said Thomas, at last.

'Doesn't matter,' said his father.

'We were looking for Towser,' said Thomas.

'You don't have to say,' said his father. 'I'm a Ketch, too.'

'Yes.'

'They flew tonight,' said Mr Ketch.

'Yes.'

'Did you see them?'

'Yes.'

'I never did. I always knew. My father told me. I would have told you one day.'

'I didn't do it,' said Thomas.

'No one else can do it,' said Mr Ketch.

There was another silence, then the embers gashed open and fell, splitting into a gold vermilion wound.

'Will Mum be all right?' asked Thomas.

'Let's get to bed,' said Mr Ketch.

They stood together and walked to the window. A faint trace of light seeped into the distant sky. It would soon be morning. Two black shapes swung round over the high roof of the Manor.

They hovered for a second, then dropped, landed delicately on the gateposts, folded their wings, and opened their mouths. Then they were rigid and still.

Mr Ketch squeezed Thomas's shoulder.

'It's the first time,' he said. 'The first time ever I saw them fly. My dad never did, nor his dad. No one remembers the last time.'

'Will she be all right?' asked Thomas.

It was the first Christmas morning that Jack and Clare had ever slept right through until seven o'clock. Jack was so tired when at last Clare woke him that he could not believe it really was Christmas.

'And we've got toboggans,' she said. 'Real ones.'

'I need that tea tray,' said their mother.

Jack squeezed her and gave his father a kiss. Then he remembered that he was too old to kiss his father and he blushed. Then he didn't care and was so pleased he kissed him again.

As soon as they had finished breakfast, they went to get Thomas.

'Me too,' he said, showing them his toboggan on the doorstep.

'Let's go, then,' shouted Jack.

'No,' said Thomas.

'Look, I'm sorry about last night,' said Jack. 'I didn't mean it.'

This was a very big statement for Jack, and Clare whistled in amazement.

'No, it isn't that,' said Thomas. 'I don't mind. I mean, we'll talk about it later. All right? I've got to go and see Mum now.'

'Half an hour,' called Mr Ketch. 'Then we're off.'

'Come on,' urged Jack.

'Not enough time,' said Thomas. 'Later.'

Mr Weever stepped out of the church and waved to them.

'Not him,' said Thomas.

'Better see what he wants,' said Jack.

'I'm staying here,' said Thomas.

'Please come,' said Clare.

So they all walked across.

'Merry Christmas,' said Mr Weever. He beamed down at them. At least, he tried to, but his was not the sort of face that could beam. He put all the things in the right places, lips, cheeks and all that, but the smile still had a sort of menace in it, a threat or a warning.

'I've got something for you,' he said. 'Come this way.'

Reluctantly they followed him. He took them through the church, past the altar and behind into a small space with steps going down to a heavy door.

'What's this?' asked Thomas, suspiciously.

'Crypt,' said Weever. 'Sort of cellar.'

127

'For wine?' asked Jack.

'No. For bodies, really.'

The children hung back.

'It's all right. This one's in two parts. There's a sort of entrance place, then another door into the burial chamber. We're only going into the first part.'

'You go first,' said Thomas.

'I'll stay here, at the top of the steps,' said Jack. 'In case I have to go and get help.'

He hated the way the vicar laughed at him, but he was determined not to go any further.

'Don't forget we were locked in the Manor last night,' he said. 'And I still don't know what you were doing there.'

'Fair enough,' said the vicar. He slid the key into the lock and turned it. There was a shuffling sound and Jack stepped back another pace.

The door opened wide. 'In we go,' said Weever. He led the other two in.

Clare shrieked. Thomas shouted.

Jack tensed, ready to run. He knew it had been a trap. He looked desperately round to see that his exit was clear. He was afraid the old man or Miss Aylmer might be blocking his escape.

'You all right?' he called down.

Then he heard Clare laugh.

'Come on, Jack,' she called.

Jack moved forward, cautiously.

A sudden howl made him jump, and he was

128

about to turn and run when a small brown and white bundle flew out of the door and threw itself at him.

'Towser!' he said.

The dog jumped up at him, licking him and danced round him.

'Towser! What are you doing here?'

'I heard a noise at the early service this morning,' said the vicar. 'And when I investigated I found him in here. I came straight to find you. Didn't want to let him out in case he ran away again.'

'How?' asked Jack. 'How could he get in when it was all locked?'

'Isn't it a mystery?' said the vicar. His face was a perfect mask of innocence. 'I expect we'll never know. Lots of strange things happening here all of a sudden.'

'Ever since you arrived,' said Jack.

'Is that so?' said Weever. 'Well, I never.'

'I've got to go,' said Thomas. 'I'm really pleased Towser's all right,' he said to Jack.

'About last night,' said Weever.

'Yes?' said Clare.

'Just one or two things we ought to talk about, I think,' he said. 'Do you think you could all come to tea with me and Miss Aylmer?'

'No,' said Jack.

'What time?' said Thomas.

'Soon as it gets dark. When you've finished

sliding down the Barrow.'

'We'll be there,' said Clare.

'Good.'

The ward was bright and cheerful, with decorations over the beds and music playing. Thomas felt better about it. But he still hated seeing his mother lying there.

'I'm feeling a lot better,' she said.

She was delighted with his present. She unwrapped it carefully, the way she always did, trying not to tear the paper.

'It's lovely,' she said.

Mr Ketch held her hand. Thomas told her about going to the Barrow after lunch with the toboggans.

'You'll be careful, won't you?'

'Yes.'

Thomas wondered whether to tell her about the night before, but his father took the decision away from him.

'They're flying again,' he said.

Mrs Ketch looked at Thomas.

'I didn't do anything,' he said.

'I don't think we've seen the last of it,' said Mr Ketch.

Thomas said nothing about breaking into the Manor.

'You haven't opened your other present,' he said.

Mrs Ketch took the small package with the dragon paper and split it open. It was fastened too carefully for her to unwrap it without damaging the paper.

'What is it?' asked Thomas.

'Have a look.'

It was a small stone, carved in the shape of a wyvern, wings outstretched. The features were worn and blunt. There was a jagged edge at the base which showed that it had been broken off from something larger.

'It's from the Kych Stone,' said Thomas.

Mr Ketch took it. 'Are you sure?'

'No. But it looks like it. See? It's been snapped off.' He ran his finger over the jagged edge.

'She wouldn't do that,' said Mrs Ketch.

'No,' agreed Thomas. 'I don't suppose she would. She must have got it some other way.'

Mrs Ketch put it on the cupboard by her bed, then thought again, and took it down and held it in her hand. It was comfortable there. She liked it.

The words on the Kych Stone came into Thomas's head:

Reach out and touch this carved stone
If you are sick and would be whole.

'When are you coming home?' he asked. He had promised himself he would not ask her that, but

131

he had not been able to stop himself.

'I can't say,' she said. She looked at her husband, who nodded. 'Sometimes,' she said, 'people don't come home again.'

Thomas looked away.

A passing nurse smiled down kindly at his freckled face.

FIFTEEN

The old man, Parcel, and Ted and Nigel, sat in the stone circle and watched the dawn. They were cold, wet, stiff and trapped. Ted and Nigel were frightened. The old man was angry.

As soon as the sky was fully light, the dogs stood up, turned away and walked off, leaving the three men free to leave.

A black figure stepped through the snow towards them, cloak trailing. He came up to the edge of the circle but did not walk inside.

'Parcel?' he called.

The old man went over to him. They faced each other from inside and out, through the gap between two stones as if through a doorway.

'What do you want?'

'You're beaten,' he said.

'Not yet.'

'I think so.'

'Wait and see.'

'We know about you now. We know you're here.'

The old man shrugged. 'Makes no difference,' he said.

'Thomas Ketch has woken the wyverns. You might as well clear out.'

'Oh, I'm going,' said the man. 'But I'll be back. I'll get the book.'

'It's Thomas Ketch's book,' said Weever. 'It's not for you.'

'No,' said Parcel. 'It's Kych's book. That's a different thing altogether. I'll be back for it.'

'Not while the wyverns are watching. They'll be alert now.'

Parcel gave Weever a contemptuous look. 'They're always alert,' he said. 'Always were. Why else would I want the book?'

Weever walked away. When he was out of sight, Parcel gave Nigel a kick. The security guard groaned in his sleep.

'Get out,' said Parcel. 'I've finished with you. Don't let me see you again.'

'What about our pay?' said Ted.

Parcel swung a fist at him and struck him on the cheek.

'Come on,' said Nigel. 'We're going.' He led Ted out of the stone circle.

'Call this Christmas?' complained Ted when they were out of Parcel's hearing.

Nigel smiled slowly. 'It is, too,' he said. 'And we're free of that old devil. Let's go and celebrate.'

'He'll follow us,' warned Ted. 'He'll get us put back into prison.'

Nigel smiled again. 'No, I don't think so. I think he's finished with us. Let's go and have a Christmas.'

'Right,' said Ted, with some relief. 'Here, did you see those things in the sky last night?'

The toboggans were heaven.

Towser leaped and danced round them as they sped down the slope of the Barrow.

'It's getting faster,' shouted Clare.

It was. As the runners packed down the snow, it got harder and smoother and slipperier, and the toboggans skidded down so fast that all three of them squealed in panic-stricken delight.

Towser slipped and he slid down the slope on his side, yapping and scrambling for a foothold.

He landed in a drift of soft snow and had to dig himself out.

'Good old lad,' said Jack as he hauled the dog back to steady ground. 'Good old lad. You'd never get lost in the Barrow, would you?'

'Or in the crypt,' said Clare.

'That's right,' said Jack. 'There was no way he could get in there. It was locked.'

'He put him in there,' said Clare. 'Weever. He must have.'

'Yes,' said Jack. He fixed Thomas with a stare. 'So I don't see why we should go and have tea with him. Not if he stole my dog.'

'He wanted us to look in the Manor,' said Clare.

'That's right,' said Thomas, who was reluctant to join in. 'I saw him coming out that night the dogs all barked. He set them off to make us think about it. I'm sure he did.'

'Let's forget him, then,' said Jack. 'Go home for tea.'

'Can't,' said Thomas.

'Why not?'

'Last night,' said Thomas. 'I still don't know what happened. They can tell us.'

'He's right,' said Clare.

'Nothing happened,' said Jack. 'We got locked in the Manor by some old man, and then the vicar and that American woman let us out.'

'What about the wyverns?' said Clare.

'That was a mistake,' said Jack. 'We imagined it.'

'All of us?' said Clare.

'It was dark,' said Jack. 'Something caught fire. There were snakes about. We got confused.'

Clare looked at her brother with blank disbelief.

'It's getting dark,' said Thomas. 'Are you coming?'

'No,' said Jack. 'I'm going home.'

The uneasy truce between the boys was breaking down. Thomas dragged his toboggan away from the Barrow. He had to walk a long way round to avoid going through the standing stones.

'Wait!' called Clare. 'I'm coming.'

Towser bounded along with them.

'Towser!' called Jack, but the dog ignored him and stayed close to Thomas. 'Towser!'

It was quite dark when they reached the village green. Thomas and Clare were there first, and they waited for Jack to catch up with them. He kept his face turned away and made straight for his own house.

Thomas knocked at the door of Viviper Cottage.

'Just the two of you?' asked Miss Aylmer in her harsh voice. 'Where's the other angel?'

'He's not coming,' said Clare.

'Afraid of the snakes?' she said, showing them

into the warm parlour.

Weever nodded a greeting. He was sprawled in a huge armchair that he still managed to make look too small.

'No. Not that,' said Thomas. 'He just isn't interested.'

'And I cleared my friends away specially for him,' said Miss Aylmer.

Thomas noticed that the room was back to its more conventional state, the way it had been the night of the carol singing. All the glass tanks were missing. A big and very interesting tea was spread out on a table. There were sandwiches and cakes and biscuits and buns and bowls of something with cream on the top.

'Not interested in what happened last night?' said the vicar. 'He sees the wyverns fly all the time, does he?' And he gave his huge laugh.

'No,' said Thomas. 'And he says they didn't fly last night either.'

'Help yourself,' said Miss Aylmer, giving everyone a plate.

Weever didn't hold back. He lunged forward and stacked his plate with at least two of everything. Before he fell back into his chair, he picked up a log and tossed it on the fire, making more sweet smoke swirl up.

Thomas and Clare took rather less.

'Did they fly?' asked Clare.

'Up to you,' said Weever. 'What do you think?'

'Yes,' said Thomas firmly.

'It's the Jacks of this world that keep what happened last night a secret,' said Miss Aylmer.

'What do you mean?' said Clare, ready to defend her brother.

'I mean,' she said, 'that this village has been pulled apart for hundreds of years, thousands perhaps. Parcel's Stones have been a centre of something very nasty. And the Barrow is the centre of something very good. I mean that Jane Gwyer disappeared because she was trying to do something important here and it went wrong. I mean that the Kych Stone tells us that there are more ways of healing sickness than the ones they know about at the hospital.' Thomas listened intently to this, but he did not interrupt. 'I mean,' she went on, impatiently, 'that the wyverns have flown here for all that time but that people prefer not to believe it, even when they see it for themselves. People's ability to tell themselves lies never fails to amaze me.'

She came to a sudden halt and took a fierce bite out of a sandwich.

Weever laughed again. 'Should I help out?' he asked.

'Yes, please,' said Thomas.

'What we know for certain,' he said, '(although everything that Felicity says is true, it is lost in time for the most part) is that there was a tradition of healing people in Herpeton, and that it

139

had something to do with ancestors of young Thomas, whose name was Kych. And that it had a lot to do with animals and with wild animals not being dangerous or frightened. It had something to do with the Manor and with the Gwyer family, who always had a way with animals. It tells you that on Jane Gwyer's monument. I expect you've noticed.'

Clare and Thomas nodded.

'But, and here's the point about last night, there's always a dark side, always a struggle. If the Kychs and the Gwyers were using that closeness to the animals to make people better, it was also possible to use it to have power over other people, and power over animals. And there were others, the Parcels, who did that. So the Barrow and the Stones stand for the two opposing sides.'

'Old Harry said that the old man was Parcel,' said Clare.

'That's right,' said Miss Aylmer. 'They're back. But Thomas here fought them off.'

'I didn't,' said Thomas.

'No one else did,' said Weever. 'And only you could.'

'But how?'

'Now, if we knew that, we'd be a lot better off,' said Weever. 'You see, in the old days, there were special things you had to do to make the wyverns fly. Words to say, actions to perform. You managed it somehow without all that.'

'Is that in the book?' asked Clare.

'Good girl,' said Weever.

'That's Master Kych's book,' said Miss Aylmer.
'Whoever gets that will be able to do what they
want in Herpeton.'

'And further afield,' warned Weever.

'Can I do other things?' asked Thomas.

'What things?' asked Miss Aylmer. Somehow
she managed to make her harsh voice sound
kind.

'Can I make Mum better?'

There was a long pause.

'I've done what I can,' said Miss Aylmer. 'With
the wyvern from the Kych Stone. We'll have to
wait and see.'

'Where did you get that?' asked Thomas.'Did
you break it off?'

'No. It's been in my family for a long time.'

'Will it work?'

'Who knows? It might.'

'At least we beat them,' said Clare. 'We won.'

'What?' said Thomas.

'Last night,' she said. 'You got the wyverns out
and we won. We'll be all right now. It's all over.'

'They'll be back,' said Weever. 'And they'll still
be looking for the book. We'll have to keep
together if we want to beat them for good. Will
you help?'

Thomas looked at him. 'I don't know,' he said.

141

'Why not?' asked Clare.

Thomas paused before answering. 'I don't trust you,' he said to Weever. 'I still don't know what side you're on, really.'

Weever was silent.

'That snake on your arm,' he said. 'Parcel had one on his. Just the same.'

Clare was angry. 'So what?' she said. 'It doesn't mean anything.'

'You make Mum better, and then I'll trust you,' said Thomas. He stood up, put his plate down and left. Clare ran after him.

They crossed the village green and paused in front of the statue of Jane Gwyer. Her calm eyes stared out blindly over the snow-covered fields.

'Make her better,' said Thomas. 'Please make her better.'

His father was waiting for him when he got home.

'Come on,' he said. 'We'll be late at the hospital. Let's see how your mum is.'

'Is it over?' asked Thomas. 'Is she better?'

'Not yet. Let's hope.'

Jane Gwyer stood stone-still and watched them drive away.